The Bandit

Center Point
Large Print

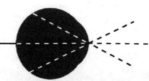

**This Large Print Book carries the
Seal of Approval of N.A.V.H.**

WEST OF THE BIG RIVER

The Bandit

*A Novel Based on
the Life of Sam Bass*

JERRY GUIN

CENTER POINT LARGE PRINT
THORNDIKE, MAINE

This Center Point Large Print edition
is published in the year 2021 by arrangement with
Western Fictioneers.

The text of this Large Print edition is unabridged.
In other aspects, this book may vary
from the original edition.
Printed in the United States of America
on permanent paper.
Set in 16-point Times New Roman type.

ISBN: 978-1-63808-051-0

The Library of Congress has cataloged this record
under Library of Congress Control Number: 2021939718

The Bandit

CHAPTER 1

Dust stirred by passing horses' hooves lingered in the air and mixed with the scent of a bright spring morning as the buzz of the crowd gathering on Hickory Street grew louder. Men shook hands, slapped shoulders, and gave an occasional laugh. A woman's voice rose to a high pitch as she yelled admonishment to some screeching children while a teenager hawked five cent apple turnovers from Maggie's Café. The crowd was there to witness the hanging of convicted murderer Claude Radkin.

Inside the confines of the drab Denton, Texas jail, twenty-two-year-old Sam Bass had just walked into the cell block to pick up the prisoner's breakfast dishes. The dark-haired youth, of average height and lean of frame, always had a smile on his face and was friendly and likeable.

Claude Radkin, the only inmate in the jail, sat on a bunk in his cell. A small ten inch by ten inch barred window above the bunk, at head height, served as an air vent while allowing the outside noise within.

The man sat with head bent down, lost in thought while he stared at the floor and waited for the deputies to come for him. He was morose and resigned to his fate. His time was almost up. Claude had killed a man in a six-gun shooting over a card game, in the resulting trial he had been found guilty and sentenced to hang. When he was arrested, Claude had said it was self-defense, that Jack Sterns, a card dealer at Denton's Red Horse Saloon, had gone for a gun when Claude shot him. However, no weapon was found on or near the body.

The prosecutor, a local lawyer named Mortimer Ames, was a short, cocky man, suited, vested and confidently intent on making a speedy trial as he commanded the attention of the courtroom audience. After thirty minutes of testimony from witnesses, Ames wasted no time and called Radkin to the stand to give his version of the incident. When the moment was right, the lawyer demanded, "Do you have any remorse for shooting and killing Jack Sterns?"

Claude fidgeted on the hardwood chair. He looked from side to side as if searching for an expected savior to come to his aid. The room remained in hushed silence, a silence unbroken by the swishing of half a dozen handheld fans that the glum-faced audience busied. Radkin sucked in a deep breath, expelled it and sat still, seemingly lost in thought. Suddenly he straightened his shoulders and turned to face the lawyer and blurted, "I ain't sorry that I shot the son-of-a-bitch. He was cheating!"

The jury comprised of townsmen and local

farmers took only minutes to register a guilty verdict.

Claude was sentenced to hang, the date of execution being today, July 10, 1873, at 11:00 a.m., exactly one week after the trial.

Now, Sam Bass stood just outside the cell bars and asked, "Can you slide me that tray under the bars, Claude?"

Claude Radkin jerked his head up at the intrusion. Turning to face the young man, he said, "Yeah, sure." He stood, picked up the tray from a nearby table then took a step, bent at the waist and slid the tray to Sam's reach.

Sam stood back while Claude went back to his cot. "Is there anything I can do for you, Claude?" he asked.

Claude was fifteen years older than Sam and had been on the wrong side of the law since he was a youngster of nineteen. He had grown accustomed to Sam's daily visits even if it was only to bring him meals or empty the slop bucket and leave after a few minutes. They were on a first name basis. Claude had even begun to feel a kinship to the young man because no one else came around.

Claude didn't move or acknowledge the question for a long moment, and then he looked over at Sam and gave a faint smile. "The only thing anyone can do for me right now is to convince the hangman to give me a proper high drop! I hope the sheriff knows what he's doing, if he's the one to spring the trap."

Sam looked at Claude questioningly.

Claude snorted. "Ain't you ever seen a man hanged?"

Sam shook his head from side to side. Claude attempted a thin smile that turned into a grimace. "Lots of things to consider when a man is strung up. If he's just hauled up and the end of the rope is tied off, he'll just strangle. I saw it done to a fella caught rustling, one time down in El Paso. It wasn't pretty! They put him on a horse, pulled the rope tight and tied the end off to a tree trunk, then slapped the horse away. That poor bastard gave a gurgled cry as soon as the horse bolted from under him, then the noose got tight and he got quiet, couldn't breathe, I expect. He kicked some and squirmed around. His face got all screwed up and turned purple. His tongue stuck out and his eyes bulged, then one of his legs gave a last kick and he pissed his pants. The whole thing only took three or four minutes. It seemed longer to me, though, before he quit moving and just hung there swinging back and forth."

"You shouldn't be thinking about those things right now, Claude," Sam said in an attempt to console the condemned man.

"Why shouldn't I think about it?" Claude flared. "Listen to 'em out there. You'd think it was the social event of the year! Hanging is a sorry way to go, whether it's a lynching or done from a gallows and supposedly cleaned up for the benefit of the ladies in the crowd. A hangman that's any good at it will place the noose around the neck and draw it snug, positioning the knot right behind the left ear." Claude touched a finger to his left ear to illustrate. "When they spring the trap and the poor bastard reaches the end of his rope the sudden jolt will snap the neck kinda sideways and break it instantly. That's if there's plenty of rope and they give you a good high drop. It's over in a matter of seconds." His voice faltered and trailed off, then he added, "So they say." Claude shook his head. "I think that I'd rather be shot! Fact is, I expected to be shot many a time when I was robbing. Guess I was luckier in them days than I am now." His voice trailed off again.

"Sounds like you were happy about robbing," Sam said.

Claude straightened up and nodded his head. "A man's got choices in how he lives. When I was your age I thought I was tough and smart, too smart to work on a hardscrabble farm night and day for damned little pay. So I beat the hell out of a stingy neighbor that had offered me a single dollar after I spent three long days of labor filling his corn crib. I took what money he had in his pockets and a couple of his best horses then rode like hell. It gave me a start. It seemed to me, at the time, that I'd never do another day's labor for wages and I never did. You are what you think you are. I chose robbing to make my way. There's nothing I can do to change that and I'm not sure I would even want to. I liked what I did and I never intentionally shot anyone while I was holding them up. I did shoot Jack Sterns on purpose, though, and now I've got to pay for it. The only thing that galls me is to have to die for killing a skunk that needed shooting!"

"Are you afraid to die, Claude?"

"No, I ain't afraid to die!" Claude was quick to answer. "I used to think I was, then one day a man in a Taos saloon, a big nasty-looking guy, decided he would change my looks. Didn't like 'em, he said. Before I could even think about anything, he had me wedged up against the bar. He pulled a long-bladed knife out and smiled while he showed it to me. I thought I was a goner. I was pretty scared and didn't know what to do, but you know what? I took the knife away from that big bastard and stuck it in his belly. He died on the saloon floor, quivering like the hog he was. After that I never worried about a damned thing. I quit worrying about being killed by anyone and things got easier. I ain't seen a man yet that I was afraid to go up against, gun or knife. Everybody's going sometime. The date of your death doesn't matter. When your time's up, it's up, that's all there is to it! It's the matter of how that's worrisome!"

Sam stood to one side when two deputies

accompanied by a skinny, balding man holding an open Bible came into the cell block. Claude did not utter a word. He rose from the bunk and stood while the deputies manacled him then led him out the cell door and through a door into the sheriff's office.

Sam picked up the tray and necessary bucket then stepped from the cell block into the office. The deputies eyed him warily as he walked quickly past them while carrying the used goods outside. Sam could hear some muffled talk begin from behind the closed door but it faded to nothing as he stepped away.

Once inside the sheriff's office, Claude spoke. "What's that kid do besides bring meals and swamp the jail?"

Sheriff W.F. Egan looked at Claude questioningly. "You mean Sam? He works for me. Does some odd jobs that keep the deputies free to do more important work."

"He seems too mild-mannered to be working in a jail," Claude said.

Egan nodded. "I didn't hire him on merit. I just saw a young man down on his luck and needing a hand to get up before he went off in the wrong direction. I remember when he first came to town. One day I was summoned over to the mercantile because they say he stole a pickle out of a barrel. Virgie Olsen, the owner's wife, wanted me to throw him in jail."

Claude smirked. "You'd throw him in jail because he was hungry?"

"No, I would have lodged him there, if I figured that he took the pickle and ate it but didn't pay for it. Sam said he didn't take it and there wasn't any evidence to show otherwise despite Mrs. Olsen's rant that she saw him eat it. I paid for the pickle and hired him instead. If I hadn't given him a way to earn his keep, then it would be of no great surprise that he might end up like you have, Claude!"

"That was mighty decent of you, Sheriff," Claude said. "Does that mean that he doesn't have any money?"

"Yeah, I suppose it does," Egan said, "though he's been here for a while, he might have squirreled away a little by now."

"He ain't a regular deputy then?" Claude asked.

"No, he's not a deputy and I don't expect he ever will be. I don't think he has the temperament for it. Like you said, he's pretty mild-mannered. Sam just does some work for me and helps around the jail when I need him to," Egan said.

"What are you going to do with all my stuff afterwards?" Claude asked.

Egan flashed a stern glare. "What you owned will be sold and the proceeds will go toward your funeral."

"Burying don't cost that much," Claude protested. "When you checked me in here I had

$132.00 and some change, a horse, saddle and bags, a converted .44 new army model Colt and a Henry rifle. I want to give it all to Sam, the kid."

"What?"

"I want the kid to have my things," Claude repeated. "List it on a paper and I'll sign it. The preacher here can be a witness. All I need is a ten dollar pine box. You ought to give the gravedigger a few dollars and five dollars to the reverend here so's he can say a few words over me when it's all done. Everything else goes to the kid. Maybe it'll give him a start and he won't have to empty your shit buckets."

When the hour for the hanging grew near, Claude was marched glumly through the street with the deputies stepping alongside, one on either side of the condemned man. They led him up the thirteen steps and now Claude alone stood on the trapdoor of the gallows. Sam watched from a distance. A hush came over the crowd when the trapdoor dropped under Claude's feet. Sam had not thought to look to see if the knot of the rope had been placed on the side of Claude's head like he had said would be best. It must have worked, though, for there didn't seem to be any movement by Claude afterwards except for his body swaying back and forth. They left him hanging for about ten minutes, all movement or swaying had stilled before two men lowered

Claude's body down and into a waiting coffin, then slid the box inside a wagon bed.

Sam was surprised and elated when Sheriff Egan called him into the office and presented him with one hundred fifteen dollars and thirty-two cents in cash, a .44 caliber Henry rifle, a .44 six-gun that took the same shells as the rifle, and a cartridge belt and holster for the six-gun. Egan directed Sam to claim Claude's horse, saddle, and saddlebags at the livery . . . the entirety of Claude Radkin's estate.

Sam was grateful for what Claude had done. He hurriedly took the items back to his bunk in the tack room and admired the guns. He was giddy with excitement as he examined his newfound fortune and didn't bother to attend Claude's funeral, not that he would have anyway, nobody else did. It was not a funeral with mourners, just a quick burial. The gravediggers had hauled the coffin out to the graveyard right after the hanging and filled in the grave before ol' Claude was even cold. Sam thought about it later and shrugged.

"Hell, dead is dead," he mused. After months of living on the lam and doing the worst menial jobs offered just to get a meal, he now had a horse and guns and money.

He felt like a rich man.

CHAPTER 2

Sam had come into Texas by way of Rosedale, Mississippi where the young man had spent six months working as a laborer in a sawmill to grub out a living. He wasn't looking to return to that part of the country. Those folks over there were still reeling from the war effort that had taken what wealth they had. Most were as poor as he was and just trying to get by.

He had saved a little of his earnings from the mill, despite his newfound fondness for gambling, and was able to buy a horse, a saddle, and an old, well-used, two dollar army Colt .44 cap-and-ball six-gun. His thirst for adventure found him searching for a way to live a life other than the mundane, daylight to dark toil on his uncle's Indiana homestead farm. He had run away from the farm and wandered aimlessly from farms to towns doing odds job for food and shelter.

Weeks and months slipped by as he traveled down the Mississippi River until one day he landed the job in the Mississippi sawmill. He spent six months putting in long hours shoveling sawdust and stacking boards. It afforded him money to live on but didn't satisfy the itch for excitement.

Sam hoped to fulfill his long-held dream of living a life on the range and becoming a cowboy. Each payday he bought at least one item of the gear he figured was needed. After six months Sam's outfit was complete and he was as ready as he was going to get, so he quit the sawmill job and headed west into Texas cattle country.

He drifted along and eventually found work on The Double D ranch near Denton, Texas. Since Sam was a greenhorn to cattle ranching, he was assigned the work of all young newcomers: cook's helper at meal times. Otherwise he spent his days mucking out stalls, slopping hogs, mending fences, and general maintenance. Sam didn't back up from any job he was assigned to and worked hard at whatever he did.

When he was finally allowed to get into the saddle for cattle duties it was in the cold of winter when others whiled away their days sitting by the fire. He rode fence lines and property lines searching for distressed or wandering cattle and shooed them back to their expected range. The long hours of riding and dismal work was just as monotonous and isolated as it was back on his uncle's farm.

By the time winter was about done, Sam was growing disillusioned. His dreamed up ideas of being a cowboy and the actuality of this job did not match up. He hung on there for the spring and summer, gaining firsthand knowledge of the roundup, the branding and castrating of the yearlings, and the ever needful fence repairs. He spent his off time enticing other ranch hands into nightly card games.

His quest for a different kind of gambling was leading him on a perilous path.

Sam had conjured up a horse race using ranch stock, much to the disdain of Jack Hinds, the foreman. Afterwards, Hinds called a halt to any future races using Double D horses.

"Either one of the riders or one of the horses might get hurt," he said sourly. No more was said about the matter, although thereafter the surly foreman kept an extra watchful eye on Sam's daily activities. Sam contented himself with the nighttime card games. Sam was always lucky with cards and soon other players were getting harder to convince to sit in on a game even if the stakes were minimal.

When fall was in the air, Sam figured to move on, he'd been on the ranch a full four seasons and wasn't longing to repeat any one of them. He was eating three times a day but he wasn't particularly happy, so he drew his pay and left without complaint from the foreman.

Sam rode into Denton, checked his horse into Work's Livery, and lodged himself in Martin's Hotel. Sam figured that since he had been so lucky at cards back at the ranch, he would give the cards a try as a source of income. The Red

Horse Saloon was a popular spot for drinkers and gamblers. Within a week, Sam had become a regular. He favored a nice cigar and branded whiskey, he was confident and was able to win a few hands but not getting much ahead. After a few days he wasn't able to hold his own at the tables against the professional dealers. His luck had turned for the worse, it seemed.

He awoke one morning with a pounding headache. He got out of bed and stooped over a wash basin sitting atop a bureau to splash some water on his face. Thoughts of last night flooded his memory, one thing he knew was that he had drunk too much whiskey and then had been foolish enough to stay in that game.

The game had seemed friendly enough. Seven card stud, jacks or better to open. He believed he was doing okay for a while, he'd won or been allowed to win a few smaller pots, enough to keep him in the game and hopeful. He played for hours until he was dealt a hand that really got his attention. It was late at night, he remembered that.

On the opening deal, Sam had received two queens as hole cards and a jack face up. A man across from him opened with an ace showing. The man to his left was showing a seven and the dealer had a king facing up. Sam was glad that he didn't have to open, that would have telegraphed his hand.

Ace bet a dollar, everyone stayed. By the time six cards had been dealt Ace bet five dollars with a pair of tens, a three and the ace showing. The dealer raised five dollars with two kings and two eights showing, Sam called but fretted. He had the two queens in the hole and a third one showing along with a five, a seven, and a nine. Ace's two pair wouldn't even beat his three of a kind but what was the dealer going on? The idea that he had a third king or third eight in the hole was worrisome to Sam. The man on the left dropped out.

Sam was holding his breath when the last card came out. His heart thudded when he peeked at his third card in the hole. It was another queen! With the one queen showing, he now had four queens. This hand would be hard to beat.

Ace checked. Sam almost smiled, the man hadn't got his full house so he was afraid to bet. The dealer, however, quickly made a bet of ten dollars.

The bet didn't surprise Sam. He looked at his hole cards again for assurance. Yep, he had four queens, and four queens would beat the full house that he suspected the dealer had. He called the ten dollar bet and raised another ten. Ace dropped out. The dealer pushed out ten dollars then said, "And I'll raise you fifty dollars!"

Sam was suddenly bewildered. He already had thirty-four dollars, more than a month's pay, lying in the middle of the table but he was certain that he had the winning hand. He sat for a moment then began counting the money he had on the edge of the table before him. Six dollars was all he came up with. He searched his pockets and found twenty-two dollars.

He said, "I've got twenty-eight dollars left."

The dealer glared at him. "If you can't call the bet, then you have to forfeit the game," he said matter-of-factly. When Sam didn't reply, the man shrugged his shoulders, then asked, "You got any goods, things like a watch or a six-gun that you might want to throw into the pot? Something that has a worth of twenty-two dollars to cover the bet, I'm willing to listen."

Sam swallowed hard as a bead of moisture began to trickle down the side of his face. "I have a horse and saddle over at January's livery. The horse is worth all of that."

The dealer looked down at the table and smiled. "So you say." He hesitated, then said, "All right, I'm willing to take on the horse, though a horse costs money to keep."

"The bill is caught up," Sam assured him.

The dealer sat back and let his eyes gaze around the room. "Very well then, this man is betting his money and his horse on this hand," he announced, then turned back to face Sam. "Go ahead and show us what you got."

Sam's heart was racing. He felt a throbbing at

his temples. He concentrated to keep his hand from shaking when he laid his cards down, face up, showing the four queens.

The small audience that had gathered around the table murmured. "I figured he had something good," one man said.

"It was well hidden," said another.

The dealer sat, seemingly unmoved, then reached out nonchalantly and turned his hole cards over.

Sam's heart thudded harder. He couldn't believe it, the man had four kings! He had two kings hidden in the hole just like Sam's three queens were. Sam was stunned and speechless. He had lost. He stood to leave when the dealer pushed a coin across the table. "Have a drink on me," he said, then turned and busied himself scooping up the money from the middle of the table.

Sam had stumbled back to his room and collapsed on the bed to sleep fitfully. Then it was morning and reality began to set in. Sam sat back down on the bed so he could put his boots on. He had no idea what the day would bring. Thankfully he had paid for his room a week in advance and it wouldn't be due again for one more day. He could spend one more night, then he would have to leave. The only things he owned were his clothes and his old six-gun. Hell, he didn't even own a horse any longer, so he couldn't even leave town unless he wanted to walk.

He thought about getting out to the ranch to see if he could get his old job back but discounted that idea. Sure, he would eat, but it wouldn't be long before he would be scheming a way to leave again. He didn't feel like groveling and besides Jack Hinds most likely wouldn't take him back anyway. No, he'd been busted before, he'd just tough it out, he figured.

It was that afternoon that the pickle incident came about. Sheriff W.F. Egan was fifty-two years old, a heavy-bodied man but not over-weight. He had just a little paunch in his belly and a little gray in his light brown hair, to go along with a happy face with a walrus mustache. From a distance he gave the appearance of the perfect grandfather, his mild manner attracted the ladies, and kids loved him and affectionately dubbed him "Dad Egan." Up close, his coolness in handling the duties of the sheriff's office made him popular with the merchants around town and those on the sly knew to be wary. One look into the man's eyes disclosed the sincerity registered there. When he spoke, he meant what he said. W.F. Egan liked being sheriff and he took the job seriously.

Sam had watched as the sheriff handed a coin to the woman in the store. "That should cover it," he said, then took Sam by the elbow and steered him out the door before Virgie Olsen could object. Sheriff Egan marched Sam to the middle of the street then stopped abruptly, standing to face Sam.

"I didn't take that pickle, Sheriff," Sam claimed. "I was just standing there thinking on buying one. I've got a few coins in my pocket."

"I didn't say you did," Egan said, "but it's ended now, so let's put it behind us. I knew when you came into town and I know you've been lounging over at the Red Horse Saloon. I also heard that you lost everything you own in a game last night, there are no secrets in this town."

The dark-haired, dark-eyed young man stood five foot eight and weighed a hundred forty pounds. He was full grown at twenty-two years but had a much younger appearance. Sam stood silently with eyes cast down as he absorbed the truth of what the lawman had said.

Egan paused for a moment, then said, "Now here's the deal. I need someone to do some odd jobs for me, maybe do a little freight loading and hauling. The pay is as good as army pay, fifty cents a day and two meals a day over at Marcie's restaurant, I have a tab there. You can bunk in the tack room behind the freight office. You won't be working directly for the sheriff's office, unless I need you for messages and such, you'll be working for me and get paid by the E&H Freight Company. I'm the E, and Dag Homer is the H."

Sam had figured he was on the way to jail

but instead the lawman was offering him a job instead. "I don't know what to say, Sheriff."

"You don't need to say anything. I just don't aim to stand by and allow a man to do petty crimes to get by." Sam started to object, to say he wouldn't, but Egan cut in, "I want you to go over to the freight office and see Dag and tell him I hired you. He'll give you a chore to finish up the day. Afterwards, you can move your stuff to the tack room and get a meal, then see me first thing tomorrow. I might have you run a message or two, depends on what comes in by morning."

Sam settled into his new duties without question. Right after breakfast he'd check in with Sheriff Egan to see if he had need of a messenger. At times he would swamp out the Sheriff's office and occasionally the jail cells if they had been used the night before. Afterwards he would go over to the freight office to see Dag Homer and get his assignments for the day. He spent most of his time seeing to the care of the company's horses and mules, feeding, inspecting hooves and shoes, then oiling lines and traces and loading, securing the freight to be hauled or unloaded as directed.

After a time, Dag began calling on Sam to do deliveries. Sam became acquainted with the trails to most of the outlying, thicket-surrounded farms and back roads to ranches during his deliveries. Before long Sam's diligent hard work was recognized and he seemed to be accepted by town folks.

Everyone, it seemed, with the exception of Jean Olsen, the pretty teenage daughter of Milt and Virgie Olsen, the owners of Olsen's Mercantile. Sam had approached Jean on the street in an attempt to strike up a conversation. When he'd walked over to face Jean, she stood back with a blank look on her face, unsmiling as she warily eyed Sam then said "Good day," and stepped away.

Sam didn't know what to think. Maybe he looked too rough, he mused. What with dark sweat circles under his arms and his clothes having a rumpled look, he didn't blame the young woman for her reaction. Or maybe it was that her mother Virgie had poisoned the waterhole over the pickle incident. Then too, it was possible that she was troubled by her monthly miseries, Sam thought.

After that, whenever Jean spotted him on the street, she would turn on her heel and go in the other direction or cross the street abruptly to avoid any chance of the two coming face to face. Sam kept his distance and did not attempt another encounter.

His association with females was limited to the affections he received from plump Mary Beth, in an upstairs room over the Red Horse Saloon.

That didn't happen often, usually after payday when he had the dollar or two that she would ask for. The amount seemed to depend on Mary Beth's mood at the time.

CHAPTER 3

With his unexpected inheritance, Sam didn't bother to reflect on his arrival in Denton some time back and his employment by the kindly Sheriff Dad Egan. What was important to him was what was at hand right now and it did not take long for Sam to restore things to the way he wanted with the new wealth that Claude Radkin had bequeathed to him. He claimed the roan horse that had belonged to Claude and treated himself to a new set of clothes, including a Stetson hat and some sorely needed new boots.

That evening he walked back into the Red Horse Saloon, bought a cigar, a glass of fine whiskey, and played cards until late but was watchful of his money other than giving Mary Beth an extra dollar tip. He met others who shared his table and conversations in the nightly card games that followed, he befriended Frank Jackson, Henderson Murphy, and Henry Underwood.

Frank Jackson was the youngest of the group at twenty. Henry Underwood was near to Sam's age, while Henderson Murphy was considerably older. The camaraderie of these men who shared his own interest was more important to Sam than what little money moved around the table. All three men were good company to drink with and play low stakes poker games.

W.F. Egan was aware of Sam's nighttime revelry but wouldn't say anything so long as it didn't interfere with Sam's work routines.

Meanwhile Sam was growing more adventuresome in his quest for gaming opportunities and bought a chestnut-sorrel mare named Jenny that was reputed to be fast. Sam matched the horse against the best contenders the locals came up with. The result was that Jenny won the race and some quick money for Sam. Enthralled by the sudden smile of lady luck, Sam began entering Jenny in numerous races and making larger bets. The consequence was that some men with tainted reputations began showing up in town.

Sheriff Egan did not like the questioning looks he was getting from some leading citizens or the buzz on the streets about Sam's new activities and association with shady characters. He decided to have a meeting with Sam and put an end to any future gossip about Sam's relationship with the sheriff's office. After calling Sam into his office, he pointed a meaty finger for Sam to take a chair then seated himself behind his desk.

"Folks are talking," he began. "I'm the elected Sheriff of Denton County and as such, it is my job to know whatever goes on around town. There are some men with questionable motives that have come to town, drawn here because of that race horse you've acquired and the money being bet on the horses." Egan held up a hand. "I know you didn't invite them here but they're here. Denton doesn't want or need to associate with that kind of undesirables. I don't want anyone to think that I personally condone your activities or that this office has any part in the outcome of those horse races or the betting that's going on. So it comes down to this, Sam, it's either you or the horse. One of you has to go!"

The sheriff sat back and waited for a reply from Sam.

Sam was as flabbergasted as he had been when Egan first ushered him out of that mercantile to stand in the middle of the street and give him a new start. His mind was in a whirl. He liked Dad Egan and the town of Denton. Jenny had won four of the last five races and he was making good money.

Now Egan was telling him that he had to choose between selling the horse and keeping the low-paying job or quitting the job and keeping the horse. He didn't falter when he came to a quick decision but didn't look Egan in the eye as he said, "I reckon I'll keep the horse, Dad. I, uh, I'll move on out of the shanty, most likely leave town in the morning."

When Sam had left the office, Egan sat behind

31

his desk still looking at the empty chair where Sam had sat. Sam was young and impressionable, and Egan hoped that whatever guidance he had given Sam in the past was correct. As Sam's mentor, Egan did not want to experience any feelings of guilt or responsibility later on if wrongness were to cross Sam's heart. He'd given Sam a choice and Sam had chosen to take what he perceived to be the higher, easier, more exciting side of things. There was nothing more to say about it.

Henceforth, Sam would make his own way and pay for the consequences of his actions.

Sam left town the next morning with Jenny in tow. On a tip from a speculator, he decided to head north and put the mare to the test in Denison. He spent a week there before losing a race to a black stallion named Night. He'd bet heavily on Jenny. After the loss, Sam headed south to work the Dallas and Fort Worth area. He studied the horses presented for races and used restraint in the bets he placed on Jenny, he didn't have much money to wager anyway. Jenny won a couple of races that gave him a little cash, enough to merely cover expenses.

One day, while he was in the stable caring for Jenny, a man in a suit came up to stand nearby as Sam was currying the mare.

"You've got a right nice little runner there," the

man said, "though I don't see her winning all the races."

Sam wondered at the man's remarks. Was he a bettor or just a wise guy?

Sam finished with the brushing, took up a cloth to wipe the horse down. "I never expected that she would win them all, just enough to keep some money coming in."

"Sometimes the fastest horse isn't necessarily the winner," the man said.

Sam caught on right away, this man was testing to see if he would throw a race. Someone could get good odds if he bet big on a less than favored horse, and if the lesser horse should happen to win there could be a handsome payoff.

Sam's immediate instinct was anger rather than caution. He thought of yelling at the stranger for the suggestion but then after a moment he digested what the man had said.

Hell, money was money and right now the money in his pockets had rapidly dwindled.

"What have you got in mind?" Sam asked.

The stranger took a moment to look around to see if others were listening, then he stepped closer to Sam. "Saturday's race, you'll be going up against Slim Jim, a fair horse but your horse is better. Make it look good, keep her close until the very end then fade back a little. There's two hundred in it for you, if Slim Jim wins. You're staying at the Columbia Hotel?"

Sam nodded. The man leaned in again. "There will be an envelope delivered to your room after the race, later on after dark."

Sam nodded again.

The man made one final comment. "You don't know me," he said, then turned on his heel and hurried away.

Sam watched as the man went out of sight around a corner. *How odd,* he mused, *no handshake, no names.* He wasn't completely sure what the man even looked like, medium height, slim build, light colored suit, small brimmed fedora hat. The face, he couldn't say if there were any distinguishing features. He really had not looked at the man's face. The entire time the stranger was standing there talking Sam had kept his eyes on Jenny's coat as he worked on her.

Sam knew that Jenny could beat Slim Jim, he knew it as soon as the starting gun went off on Saturday. Slim Jim was slow to get going. Sam never encouraged the mare to run full out and from an observer's point of view, it was a lackluster performance. Slim Jim won by a half-length. Sam heard the catcalls from onlookers when he rode past them on his way to the stable. "Damned poor showing," one voice said, and a different voice accused, "You held that horse back!"

Sam waited in his hotel room all night, but no one came to the door and no envelope was slid under the door. At dawn, he was madder than hell but who could he chase down to demand payment? Who could he complain to? He scoured the streets for a glimpse of the well-dressed stranger to no avail. He'd been had for a chump and he felt like one, too. When he went to the stable to check on Jenny he was stopped from entering by a deputy marshal.

"Who are you and what are you doing here?" the man asked.

"My name is Sam Bass and I came to check on my horse that's boarded here. Is there a problem?"

The deputy pointed inside the stable. "A man was killed here last night, maybe you can identify him."

Sam followed the deputy inside. Near a stall lay a body. The shirt and front of the light-colored coat the man wore were covered in dried blood. He had been stabbed to death.

Sam stepped forward to view the body and did his best to conceal any recognition. "I don't know him," Sam said. "I never met him."

Afterwards, Sam figured that maybe it was time to leave this town before any association to the dead man came to light.

CHAPTER 4

It was a warm early May afternoon in 1875 when Sam Bass walked his roan down the dusty street of San Antonio, Texas. A lead rope through a D ring on the back of his saddle snugged Jenny along. He still had a little money even though he had spent more than he had planned for trail grub and camp goods and grain for the horses.

He booked a room at a hotel then took the horses to Sid's livery. Sid was a brawny man who smiled a lot. "Four bits a night each and I'll rub them down, too," he said, then added, "Ten cents more and I'll give each a scoop of grain."

"That would be fine," Sam said then fished in his pocket and handed the man a dollar and a quarter. "The grain, too. I'm apt to stay a day or two but I'll be in to pay you each day if I stay longer."

Sid smiled, handed Sam a nickel change, then led the animals away.

Sam was hot, sweaty, dusty, and tired of riding so he walked into the first saloon that he came to, The Calico Calf. There most likely wasn't five degrees difference inside the saloon than out in the sunshine, but at least the darkened interior gave one the sense of being cooler. Sam headed to the end of the room-length bar where offerings of a free lunch sat, which consisted of thin ham slices, beginning to curl on the edges and crumbly rat cheese covered by a white cloth to keep the flies off. The bartender walked right over to Sam.

"What will it be, stranger?" He nodded toward the food. "Lunch is free with the purchase of a beer."

Sam held up two fingers. "I'll take two beers for starters."

The bartender bobbed his head and walked away. He was back in no time with two mugs foamed at the top. "Ten cents," he proclaimed. Sam slid a dollar across the bar then picked up one beer and tasted it. It was semi-cool. He swigged the beer in great gulps and had drained the first mug by the time the bartender had brought his change.

Having not eaten since last night's camp Sam turned his attention to the ham and cheese. The bartender reached under the bar and brought up a bowl of boiled eggs. "Have yourself a couple," he said. "I keep 'em down here otherwise they disappear too fast."

Sam nodded and reached for the bowl. After Sam had taken two eggs the bartender placed the bowl back under the bar and walked to the other end to wait on a newly arrived customer.

After he had his fill of the free lunch, Sam took his remaining beer and walked over to sit at an empty table. Sam was sipping on his fourth beer when a man seated with two others at a table next to his table leaned over toward him.

"We're getting ready for a game of poker. Want to sit in?"

Sam glanced at the man for a moment then nodded. "Yeah, that would be fine as long as the stakes aren't too high."

"Just penny-ante stuff, nickel to open," the man said.

Sam joined them. The man had a few years on Sam but not many. He guessed him at no more than twenty-seven or twenty-eight. The other two looked about the same age. They all had the look of cattle drovers and were dressed alike in dusty and somewhat rumpled trail garb.

"Joel Collins," the man said while extending his hand. Sam repeated his own name and shook hands with Joel and the other two men, Willie Jacobs and John (Skeeter) Wilcox.

"Are you with one of the outfits around here?" Joel asked then started to deal the cards. "Five card stud," he said as Sam and the others clunked nickels for the ante onto the center of the table.

Sam took a sip of his beer. "Nah, I just got into town from up north. I came down here in hopes of finding some new opportunities."

"What kind of opportunities do you hope to uncover?" Joel asked.

"I own a pretty fast mare that I keep just for racing. I was hoping to see if there was anyone with a horse that they think could beat her," Sam said.

"Uh hah," Joel said, "a sporting man. I'd like to see that horse."

Sam nodded. "She's at Sid's Livery, a chestnut sorrel."

"Tomorrow, after breakfast," Joel said.

"That would be fine," Sam said, "I'm a little trail worn right now."

"Let me guess," Joel said, "You came down here looking for a new start because there's nothing left or waiting for you back where you come from."

Sam was a little taken back by his own transparency. Here was someone who was very perceptive and it seemed the man could look right into his head and read his thoughts.

"I reckon there's some truth to that," Sam answered.

Joel grinned. "I ain't in the business of worrying about a man's past. No offense intended. No more will be mentioned of it."

Sam nodded. "None taken." Sam didn't know what to think of Joel but he took a liking to the man.

After two hours of play everyone seemed to be holding their own, each having taken a pot from time to time while making small talk about horses and the going price of cattle in Kansas from Texas herds.

"They say that up in Ellsworth, Kansas you can get as much as eighteen dollars for a four dollar Texas steer," Joel said.

Sam could cipher as well as anyone else. "That sounds like a pretty good mark up, if you got some to sell."

"Skeeter, Willie, and I are working on that right now," Joel said, "we were out looking at some stock and talking to some ranchers today. The deal will come about and it will take a little time yet, but things are coming along pretty good."

Skeeter bet ten cents when he paired fours. Sam raised ten cents when he got a second ten to go with the one he had in the hole.

"Right after breakfast then," Joel said then began to deal again.

Sam looked up wondering what he meant. Joel could see the questioning in Sam's eyes. "We'll take a look at your horse right after breakfast."

Sam nodded. "Yeah. Sure thing."

The hand was over when Sam drew another ten giving him two of that kind showing and one in the hole. No one could best it so Sam drew in his winnings that totaled out to two dollars even in the pot. Sam felt good when he went to bed and somewhat satisfied with meeting his new friends.

Early the next morning Sam got up, put on his shirt and pants, and had just finished pulling on his boots, he stamped to seat each foot in the boots. He'd been awake for some time. A habitual early riser, he had gotten up, washed his face, and shaved. He'd taken plenty of time to put on clean clothes, folded the dirty ones into a pile to get laundered, and was ready to go downstairs to the hotel restaurant for breakfast when a knock sounded on his door.

Sam stepped to the door and opened it. Joel Collins stood in the hallway, he was cleaned up as well. From the top down Joel wore a flat brimmed, low crowned hat, a black broadcloth suit jacket over a white shirt and string tie. No vest but freshly pressed pin striped grey pants and shiny black boots. He looked like a gambler and Sam said so. "Hell, Joel, you look like a well to do gambling man."

Joel grinned broadly. "I dress this way when I work the streets, and range garb when I work horses and cattle. You ready for breakfast, Sam? Afterwards I'd like to see that fast horse you have."

Sam and Joel sipped coffee then ordered eggs, potatoes, ham slices and biscuits. "How'd you get into horse racing?" Joel asked between bites.

Sam swallowed a slurp of coffee. "I've always liked horses and gambling too. When I found out that horse was for sale, I bought it. It seemed like the natural thing to do." Sam told of the races Jenny had won in Denton.

"That sounds pretty good, Sam, how come you left there?" Joel asked.

By the time breakfast was over, Sam had told Joel all about W.F. Egan ordering him to get rid of the horse or leave town. He told about the loss in Denison. He didn't say anything about being suckered into making his horse lose a race in Fort Worth, only that he figured to leave the entire area and hopefully turn his luck in a new location. Joel had a way of allowing him to disclose things about the horse and himself that he normally wouldn't tell to others.

Afterwards, Joel paid the bill. "My treat," he said and left a generous tip for the waitress also.

They walked the short distance to Sid's Livery. Joel walked around the horse, rubbing his hands over the mare's legs. "Can we take her out? I'd like to see her run," he said.

Later, just on the edge of town after Jenny had given a good demonstration of her speed, Joel and Sam walked the mare back to the livery. "I like what I saw, Sam, you've got a good horse there. I think she could make us both some money if you'd like me to set up a race."

Sam was silent for a moment, remembering the bad experience in Fort Worth. "I'll only let her race if there is some sort of money put up as a prize for the winner. For lack of money, I can't bet enough to do me much good, even with odds."

"No problem, Sam, I'll see what I can do. I know it costs to keep that animal," Joel said. "Do you have a minimum you'd be willing to race for?"

"A hundred dollars," Sam was quick to say. "More is always better but a hundred would be a good starting figure in a new place."

It was five days later that the half mile race was set to be held with a purse of $150.00 for the winner. Joel had worked hard at convincing various merchants to contribute to the prize money. Five dollars here, ten dollars there, he'd even put twenty dollars of his own money in the pot. The owners of the other two horses slated for the race each put up twenty dollars and the saloons made up the balance. Joel figured that the real money was to be made in the betting if he could get some odds, however even money was the best he could muster. The wagering was heavy on the two local horses, particularly Joe Craig's "Lightning," a blaze faced roan. The other horse, a young gelded bay, appeared heavy but word on the street said the horse often finished well.

When the gun sounded to start the race, Lightning jumped ahead immediately and stayed there for half the race. Jenny was a half-length behind and the bay brought up the rear.

Sam urged Jenny on as the roan cow pony just ahead of her wasn't able to sustain the lead. The bay was not a problem until near the end, coming on strong to finish second just behind Jenny and Sam at the finish line.

Joel and Sam were jubilant with the win. Sam was just happy to have money in his jeans and Joel never said how much he had collected from his bets.

Sam had celebrated his previous victories lavishly enough, he figured, and had treated himself to a thick steak, some cigars, expensive whiskey and time with the ladies of the night. Joel Collins demonstrated his celebrations seeming without worry about tomorrow. He threw money away as if feeding scratch to the chickens. At first Sam perceived his friend's actions as foolhardy but soon allowed himself to throw rational thinking to the wind and joined in with reckless abandon. He'd watched as Joel freely bought drinks for strangers and any of the ladies in the saloons that came near. He would laughingly light up a big cigar, order a round of drinks for the table and foolishly call a poker bet without even looking at his hole card. "It'll all come out in the end. Cain't win if you ain't in the game!" Joel quipped while tossing money into the middle of the table, calling the bet instead of scrapping the hand.

Sam basked in the foolishness. When he trailed downstairs behind a smiling blonde of questionable age, she ran over to two other scantily clad girls near the bar. "He gave me five dollars!" she giggled. The other two women's mouths dropped open, the standard rate was two dollars.

Finally after the third night of debauchery the celebrant's body couldn't take any more. The sunlight blaring through the open window of Sam's room crossed his face and woke him to nausea. He bolted upright then reached down to the edge of the bed and took hold of a chipped chamber pot, lifting the receptacle into his lap. The smell that wafted from it to his nostrils reminded that he'd used it earlier, and that was all it took for him to puke out the acid remnants of last night's binge. He felt immediate relief, despite a throbbing headache. Sam put the pot down then flopped back onto the bed and stared at the ceiling through bleary eyes. After he had finished morning ablutions and gotten dressed, he went downstairs to the hotel restaurant to find Joel sitting at a table, idly stirring a cup of coffee.

Joel smiled on Sam's approach. "Morning, Sam. You look a little green around the gills."

Sam remained silent as he took a chair across from Joel.

"A little hair of the dog might fix you right up," Joel snickered.

Sam gratefully took an offered cup of coffee and began slurping the hot liquid.

It was a light meal of a biscuit, marmalade and

coffee for Sam, while Joel proceeded to have a full breakfast of meat, potatoes and eggs. Sam marveled at how Joel was reacting as if it was just another day with no apparent adverse effects from the past few days of carousing.

After the meal was finished, Joel sat back in his chair with his index finger hooked into a cup handle. "We need to think about the next race," he said nonchalantly. "Need to think about what would bring us the most money."

Sam brought his head up to look across the table. "What do you mean, Joel? The winning horse always pays the best."

Joel answered right back, "Not necessarily."

Sam felt a twinge of alarm. "What do you have in mind?" he asked, vaguely remembering he had asked that very thing once before.

Joel took a sip of coffee then sat the cup down. "It would be easy enough to get a rematch race. The betting would change, of course, all the betting would be on Jenny, the favorite now. No chance to make decent money unless . . ." Joel hesitated for a moment then leaned forward, lowering his voice. "Unless Jenny was to happen to lose a close race."

Sam had a certain admiration for Joel but here he was suggesting out and out cheating which Sam had conceded to before up in Fort Worth with disastrous results. That was one of the reasons he had come to San Antonio, to get away

47

from the crooks and the fixed races, to get a fresh start. "Would there be any other way?" he asked timidly.

A faint smiled crossed Joel's face. "Sure. Jenny could most likely win the race and pick up some purse money, that's if we could even get sponsors for the purse. The newness has worn off and sponsors are wary. Racing for a purse is chicken feed compared to what could be made by placing our bets correctly."

Sam nodded at the logic then spent five minutes telling Joel of the mysterious man in Fort Worth, of the offer, the subsequent race and the death of the man and—of course—the money that was never delivered.

Joel listened until Sam had finished and then shrugged. "You can get burned in this business, if you don't know who you're dealing with. This is different," he cajoled. "We're partners now and we'll share equally, gains or losses. I believe that you would not object to making some good money even if it means doing something others aren't aware of. All we have to do is to put our money on the winning horse."

Sam did not take offense at that but thought he spotted a problem. "Betting on the other horse would seem a little obvious," he reasoned.

Joel came right back. "Oh, you and I wouldn't bet against our own horse. I'd get Skeeter to do that for us. He's good for things like that. We'll put a token bet on Jenny so that everything appears legit."

Sam nodded uneasily. It made his gut roll, but with Joel's assurance, he decided to go along with the plan.

For the next few days Sam devoted his time to pampering Jenny, seeing that she got new shoes, a workout each day followed by rubdowns and measured grain. Joel busied himself setting up the race and soliciting for prize money. This had to look good, he figured, so he went about his activities with the same fervor as the first race.

Five days later the race was held on a bright sunny afternoon with the same horses due to run the same half mile distance. Joel had hawked it as a rematch grudge race. Skeeter had no problem getting all the money he offered to bet on the bay covered as smug bettors put their money on Jenny.

This second race started out the same as the first one. The roan, Lightning, jumped to a fast start with Jenny second and the bay trailing close behind. At the halfway mark, Sam urged Jenny past Lightning with the bay a little closer this time. A shouting crowd watched then groaned and cussed loudly when the bay nosed out Jenny at the finish line with the roan a now distant third. The race had gone exactly as Joel had predicted.

Afterwards Joel, Sam, and Skeeter met in Joel's

room. Skeeter handed a stack of cash to Joel. "I collected six hundred eighty two dollars!" Skeeter said.

Joel slapped him on the shoulder. "That's great, Skeeter, really good." He counted out one hundred dollars and handed it to Skeeter. "How's that?" he asked.

Skeeter smiled broadly. "I'm happy with that," he said then poked the money into a shirt pocket and left the room.

Joel separated some more bills. "Here you go, partner," he said as he handed Sam two hundred ninety one dollars, keeping the balance of two hundred ninety one dollars for himself.

Sam took the money, leafed through it and then said, "We might have a problem with Jenny."

Joel looked up. "How's that Sam? What's wrong?"

"She was favoring a front hoof when I took her back to the stable. I noticed it during the race. That bay beat us without me having to hold her back. If she's to come up lame, then we'll be out of the racing business."

Joel shrugged. "I guess we'll see how she's doing in the next few days. For now let's go do a little celebrating."

For two weeks Sam spent much time with Jenny, fretting over the mare getting no better. At the livery, Sid examined the mare's right front hoof. "Needs to be put to pasture," he noted.

Sam made a trip out to see Joe Craig at the Circle C ranch. Joe was an amiable man who loved his ranch and his horses. "I won't pay you anything for a lame horse," Joe said, "but you can leave her here, if you want, I've plenty of pasture land. Who knows, she might come out of it in time." Sam thanked the man and left.

That very evening Joel found Sam at The Calico Calf, sitting alone at a table, head down brooding. He had been drinking straight shots of whiskey. Joel walked over and took a chair. He pointed at the bottle. "That won't bring the horse back."

Sam swallowed the remnants in his glass. "I know that, Joel, I'm just sorry to see her gone." He let out a long breath. "Now I'll have to find something else to do."

Joel reached and took hold of the whiskey bottle, he tipped it up and took a swig then wiped his mouth with the back of his hand. "We've lost our cash cow but there's other ways to make money. Anyway, it's time for us to do some droving."

Sam straightened in his chair. "Droving?" Something niggled at him, something about how Joel said the word.

Joel smiled. "Do you remember when we first met and I told you that Willie, Skeeter, and I have been working on procuring enough cattle to make a drive up to Kansas?"

Sam nodded. "Yeah, I recall," he answered, wary.

Joel dipped his head a little at Sam's tone. "Well, we've been busy getting things ready and I now believe that we have enough cattle lined up, and the time is right to make a drive. We'll spend tomorrow putting the herd together then start the drive the next morning. We could use you if you want to go along."

Sam thought for a moment. This was exactly the kind of work he had wanted and expected to do when he first went to work at the Double D Ranch up near Denton. Now he was being offered a chance to redeem himself, perhaps the beginning of a profession that would last a lifetime and he could set the life of larceny aside. Since Joel seemed to be sincere in this new endeavor, Sam decided to come clean and reveal his past. He cleared his throat before speaking. "You might as well know, Joel, that I've done about everything imaginable on a farm with the handling of horses, mules and such. I spent a year on a ranch up by Denton, mostly doing cooking, fence work and gofer chores. I don't claim to be partial to ranch chores and I've never trailed a cattle herd," he confessed.

"Hell, Sam, sometimes a man's gotta do some things whether he likes it or not," Joel said. "I believe that the easy money has dried up around here so we have to do what's at hand."

Sam nodded. "I hear you there, Joel. I haven't been particularly partial to a lot of the jobs I've done, but that doesn't mean that I won't do what's necessary, in order to get by."

"Why don't you throw in with us and come along?" Joel said. "You're already an experienced ranch hand and you'll pick up in no time what needs to be done to drive the herd. What do you say?"

Sam worked the thing over in his mind. Hell, he was tired of getting drunk in San Antonio anyway. *Maybe my luck is changing for the better,* he mused. What with the extra care he had given Jenny his money had taken a hit. He decided to take his friend's offer. "Yeah, that sounds good, Joel. I'd like to tag along on your cattle drive. Starting tomorrow, you say?"

CHAPTER 5

At breakfast the next morning, the four men sat around their table sipping coffee while waiting for the meal. Joel was the first to speak. "Glad you could come along, Sam. Now here's the deal. We don't own any cattle but I've got a little money and intend to buy a few head myself, but the bulk of the herd will be from some local ranches here about. Our aim was to offer the ranch owners an opportunity to let us trail some of their cattle to Kansas for them, saving them the time and expense of the trip not to mention the hassle. It won't cost them a thing upfront, all they are putting up is a few cattle and I imagine they'll most likely throw in some culls just to clean up their home stock. Since we're not charging them anything upfront, we have to pay our own expenses and settle up after the cattle are sold."

Sam didn't say anything as he realized that this was another one of Joel's schemes that surely had some untold risk to it.

Joel must have seen the expression in Sam's eyes. "Don't worry. There's little to go wrong and if you're short of cash I can cover you until we sell the herd."

Sam didn't want to feel like he was being a burden. "I can pay my own way."

Joel smiled. "Fine, fine, now if the four of us each put up fifty dollars apiece, we'd become partners and have enough money to buy what grub we might need to get us going. Willie's already got a cook lined up, a man who has his own wagon, he said he'd do it for a hundred dollars for the trip and his two sons are coming along to help with the herd. All we have to do is supply the grub."

Sam reached into his pocket as Joel and Skeeter each laid out fifty dollars in front of Willie. "That's all I got left," Skeeter said. Sam handed his fifty dollars to Willie.

After breakfast Joel stood and turned to Willie. "Things should be getting started over at Richardson's. He said that he'd put up a couple hundred head. His men will bring them over to that pasture next to Coyote Creek."

Willie nodded. "I'll have the wagon and supplies over there before supper time."

By mid-afternoon, Nate Richardson's drovers had driven two hundred twenty-five head to the Coyote Creek rendezvous pasture where Skeeter and Sam waited. Bill Cranston's Circle C men delivered another two hundred fifty head later in the day. Joel and two men came in pushing twenty head of cattle and an even dozen horses that had been bought from another outfit. The two wranglers left once Joel's cattle and horses melded into the main herd of cattle. Before long, Willie rode in leading the way for a man who was driving a chuck wagon, with two teenaged boys riding saddle horses alongside.

By nightfall, the camp was established on one side of the creek and nearly five hundred head of cattle milled about on the grassland across the creek. The new cook, a slender man of forty-seven years, going by the singular name of "Jensen" and one of his teenaged sons quickly had strong coffee made while they put together a fine meal of fried chicken, boiled potatoes, thick gravy and corn bread. "Starting tomorrow it'll be beans aplenty!" Jensen said jovially. The sons were introduced as Spike, who was the younger of the two being sixteen years old, and Henry, a year or so older. They appeared to be chips off the block, their slim builds, rangy looks and speech emulating their father.

After supper, Joel stood while nursing his coffee. "We gotta set watches over the herd," he said. "Sam, you can relieve Willie for the first watch from now until ten. I'll come to relieve you. Skeeter will take over from twelve to two then Henry from two until four and Spike can watch them until we're ready to leave come daylight."

Joel answered Sam's questioning look. "You need to just ride around the herd real slow like, and keep 'em bunched as best you can. Keep the strays from wandering. This is all new to the cattle too, but they'll settle and bed down before long. If you see any big problems, just ride over and get me and the others."

It was an uneventful, star-filled night and for the most part the cattle seemed content to remain bunched without much prodding. At dawn, Willie rode over to where Spike sat on his sorrel. "Better go in and get some grub, your dad is already starting to gather things up so he can get going."

While Sam and all the others, except Willie, who was watching the herd, were finishing their breakfast, Joel stood and spoke to everyone. "To get started, we're going to walk our horses amongst the herd and roust them to their feet and push them a little. Slow and easy in order to not get them excited. Cattle are dumb shits and will react to any rough handling by running. We don't want that. The trick is to let the cows believe that it's their idea to move along. Once they get started, it'll just be a matter of us following along while keeping them herded up."

Sam figured the speech was for the benefit of the two Jensen boys as well as him. Joel, Willie and Skeeter had each been on at least one drive before.

Joel continued. "Jensen will take off first and

58

be waiting a ways up the trail when we're ready to give the cattle a noon rest. Skeeter and Henry will work the right flank, Willie and Spike the left flank. It's the flanker's job to keep any wanderers from dropping out, then one man can drop back to help out the drag man from time to time. Sam, you'll ride drag today, I'll show you how soon as you're ready. The thing is, just keep the strays from wandering and keep all of 'em moving. If your horse gets tired, change to another at the noon break. We're trying to do fifteen, twenty miles today."

By the time those miles had been covered Sam had firsthand knowledge of how much work it was to ride drag at the tail end of a cattle herd. He came into camp covered by a layer of dust from head to foot. He still wore a bandana around his face. He pulled the bandana off and sneezed immediately then placed an index finger to depress one nostril and shot a wad of dirt and mucus out the other then repeated the process with the other hand and nostril, wiping his fingers on his pants.

Joel sat and watched Sam's nose cleaning, seemingly unconcerned. When Sam was finished, Joel announced, "You've got the ten to midnight watch tonight."

Sam didn't say anything, his mouth was too dry, but he nodded his understanding.

Jensen cackled when Sam went to fill his dish

for supper. "Boy, you look like you've been digging for prairie dogs," he joshed.

Sam, tired as he was, tried to smile. "It's dusty as hell back of the herd."

The next morning Henry relieved Sam off drag duty. "Joel said we are to rotate every day," the youth said. "I guess you get to ride flank with Skeeter today."

Each of the riders rotated as such every day the entire trip so that each man rode drag every fifth day. All but Joel, which no one questioned. Joel was the boss of the outfit, but still participated in the watches at night. He had enough to do as it was, leading the way, finding a place to camp for the night then checking on the critters and riders. At times he would lend a helping hand to the drag rider or anyone else who appeared like they were in need of assistance.

The days to come were long and monotonous, everyone putting in sixteen to eighteen hours in the saddle. After a week, the cattle became so used to traveling they would often be up and feeding ahead of their bed ground without being prodded, before everyone had even finished breakfast. The rider on duty could do little but ride along with a watchful eye until the drovers showed up.

Every rainstorm and river crossing had a tale waiting to be told. They had lost only a few head to misfortune. Two steers drowned in river crossings, three had lamed and were left for the Indians, and two mysteriously disappeared.

Eighty-one days later they arrived in Ellsworth, Kansas.

Once the cattle were penned, Joel called out to Sam. "You can come along with me to get the money for the herd. I paid Jensen off already and gave him a twenty five dollar bonus. I gave each of his boys seventy five dollars. Jensen said he and the boys were going over to Wyoming to see his brother. Willie and Skeeter are going to sell those extra horses we have and then book us rooms over at the Drover's Cottage."

Sam watched as the suited man counted out seven thousand, eight hundred, and eight dollars, mostly in hundreds and twenties, into a stack on the table. Joel shook hands with the man on the deal at sixteen dollars a head for four hundred eighty-eight head that had been counted at the pens. When they stood to leave, Sam shook the brawny buyer's hand also, but he never did catch the man's name.

When they checked into the Drover's Cottage, Joel handed Sam five dollars. "Get us a bottle and come on up to my room," he looked at the key tag, "room eighteen, so we can divvy the money up." Sam nodded then went into a saloon and got a bottle of whiskey.

Once in the room, Sam poured a generous amount into two glasses then handed one to Joel.

Joel held the glass aloft. "Here's to good days." The two men clinked their glasses together and then took hefty swigs of the fiery liquid.

Joel sat before a small table and placed the stack of bills on it. He counted off an even four hundred dollars. "This pays me back for the horses and twenty head of cattle I bought with my own money." He put the four hundred into a shirt pocket and then picked up the larger stack and began counting as he divided the entire stack into four equal piles. When finished, Joel pushed one of the piles toward Sam. "Your share comes to one thousand twenty-seven dollars, less the sixty-nine dollars that is your part of what I paid Jensen and his boys, for a total of seventeen hundred fifty eight dollars, same as mine, Willie's, and Skeeter's."

Sam was taken aback, he had developed a growing friendship and kinship with this man. Joel was not one to shirk any kind of duty, always ready to jump in and help where needed and now he was sitting here offering to Sam one fourth of the entire sales price of the herd. He respected Joel as a leader, a fair man and thought that Joel had given him the opportunity to work at something legitimate that could possibly define his future. He had not thought about what kind of wages to expect, figuring a hundred dollars plus the reimbursement of his fifty dollar investment in grub at the beginning of the drive would have been more than fair. What was on the table was more money than he had ever seen at one sitting in his lifetime. "But I thought we had to ride back to Texas and pay off Richardson and Cranston for the cattle they trusted to us," Sam said cautiously.

Joel looked at him and smiled. "No use thinking like that, not for a man in our game. We left that behind when we took those cattle and turned into true enough bandits. Half of those cows we got from old man Richardson were stolen by him and his riders. Hell, some of them he had just rustled the night before we left! I saw the brands on the cattle. And Cranston, that old skinflint would whine if he got twenty dollars a head for the culls he pawned off on us. We did all the work! And it is a true enough fact that there ain't no honor when it comes to thieving! If those two old bastards want any of this hard-earned money, then they can just come up here and take it away from us!"

Sam was amazed and hesitant, looking first to Joel then to the pile of money as if he were torn between fair play and outright stealing.

Joel seemed unconcerned as he poured another drink. "You can take your share and ride back to Texas if you want, or you can ride with us. Personally, I didn't leave anything of value in San Antonio and I don't believe you did either, so I see no need to go back." He gestured with his glass, focusing his attention on his companion. "But you, Sam, *you* can do what you want." The smile touched his lips and then spread to his eyes, a hint of challenge lurking behind the warmth. "Bandit or petty thief," he murmured.

Sam couldn't help but like Joel, but the man was no upstanding cattleman as he had no doubt professed to Richardson and Cranston. He was clever, smart enough to trick others into trusting him. Sam was no stranger to stealing either, what with the fixed races he had done. Nor was he above taking advantage of a situation when the opportunity arose, and he figured he could get away with it.

However, he had never conjured the thoughts of long range thinking that it took to make a score as big as the one Joel had just accomplished, and though delighted by the offering of the newfound riches, he wasn't sure that being called a bandit instead of a petty thief made it any less a crime. Still . . .

Mind made up, his right shoulder hitched in a slight shrug and he reached over and took the stack of money. Smiling broadly, Sam stuck out a hand to his friend. "Reckon I'll ride along for a spell, Joel."

Joel shook hands and then stood. "I was hoping you would. Now let's get cleaned up and get to some serious drinking."

Sam, Joel, Willie and Skeeter went on a week-long binge of drunkenness and reckless gambling, outrageously giving the scantily clad, painted-up percentage girls huge tips.

Late one night, the revelry began to change as one man grew emboldened by the effects of the strong drinks he swigged. With a nickname like Skeeter, it would be easy to assume the man was a mild-mannered, easygoing sort. That may have been true on the job, but once Skeeter got a few drinks in him, he became overbearing, demanding, mean and nasty. As the evening wore on, it seemed Skeeter would purposely attempt to pick a fight with anyone over the slightest reason. An argument over card dealing grew to fisticuffs between Skeeter and the dealer. Willie stepped in when another man took the dealer's side. Before any guns were drawn, a quick-acting deputy marshal arrested Skeeter and Willie. The two spent the night in jail, paid twenty-five-dollar fines and were released. They came into the saloon around noon to find Joel and Sam sipping beer. "Looks like you two had a rough night," Joel observed.

"I should have shot that son of a bitching dealer!" Skeeter said, pulling out a chair. "Still might if he screws with me again."

"Well, you better make it quick," Joel advised, before Skeeter could even sit down. "We're pulling out soon as I get a meal."

Sam was just as surprised at this new revelation

as Willie and Skeeter. No one questioned nor argued with Joel's decision.

"Where are we going?" Willie asked.

Joel gulped the last of a mug of beer. "We're all tired of cattle driving. We ought to do something different for a spell. I've a hankering to go up Dakota way, see some new country. There's a gold strike going on up there. A poor man's gold strike is what a fellow told me. That's where a man can search the creek banks for gold by using only a shovel and a pan, just like they did out in California. No heavy equipment involved. Every damn fool and his son are either there already or on their way. They say Deadwood at night is a regular Sodom and Gomorrah."

"You sound like a preacher, Joel," Sam noted.

Joel smiled. "Yeah. Well, anyway, I was told that there are plenty of saloons, whiskey, loose women and gold money being gambled in Deadwood. I'm dying to see the place, so I figure on checking it out and seeing where Hickok was killed. Of course it's still like I've always said before, you all can do as you want, but I'm going. We can check out Ogallala on the way. I understand that the place is another trail end cow town."

The foursome made a trip to the mercantile where they bought an assortment of food items for trail cooking and camp goods, coffee pot, cups, skillets and such. They split the goods up so each man had a gunny sack of items tied behind his bedroll. There was no hurry, no deadline to meet, so they rode casually northwest into the Nebraska territory.

Four days later, in an evening camp, Sam sat by the campfire finishing a smoke and thinking about how good a shot of rye whiskey would go right now and a gambling table. The call of saloon life pleasures was getting stronger as they neared Ogallala.

Ogallala proved to be a trail end cow town full of excited cowboys roaming from saloon to saloon recklessly partying just like they did in Kansas. Sam, Joel, Willie and Skeeter stayed three nights then, unsurprisingly, Joel declared it was time to leave the city comforts and head on north. "Time's up," Joel said, "we've seen everything Ogallala has to offer and it isn't any different than Ellsworth, so I figure we ought to go on up to Deadwood."

The mornings were crisp, clear and sunny, with a wisp of high clouds slowly moving above. Later in the afternoons it would warm up to near eighty-five degrees. After two days of travel, Sam noticed that the further north they traveled the colder it was getting in the mornings, especially before daylight when the nighttime dew had formed into frost on his blanket.

It was a brisk, sunshiny October day when the foursome rode into Deadwood. Sam figured the place was the grubbiest burg that he had ever laid eyes on. It didn't appear to be much of a town that was built in a gulch. The middle of the single street was deep in mud with ditches, holes, manure and tree stumps. One and two story frame buildings snugged together on both sides of the roadway.

Any cattle town had this place beat in appearance, Sam figured. Hell, even Skiddy Street, built in a ravine in the low end of town, down in Denison, Texas, had a better daytime appearance than this. But the street was busy, teams and wagons slogged along up and down its length, some were stopped, their owners in various modes of loading or unloading boxes, crates and goods of all sort. Boardwalks were full of men dressed in woolen work clothes, their heavy boots clomping the boards as they moved along.

No one paid the four new arrivals any attention. With all the activity on the street there was no room to tie their mounts to a hitch rack so they rode around until locating a livery and checked the horses in. Afterwards, they walked to the first saloon they came to, The High Grade. The saloon was already lively, smiling girls working the floor, gaming tables operating and a piano player plinking out a familiar tune off to one side. They took seats at an empty table and ordered a bottle and four glasses. Skeeter flipped out a five dollar gold coin to pay for it. "I'll buy the first round," he said. "I need something to warm me up, I liked to froze last night."

The bartender looked at the five dollar gold piece. "It's ten dollars for the bottle," he said matter-of-factly.

Skeeter frowned then produced a second five dollar gold piece. "How much is it for a glass of beer?" he asked sardonically.

"Two bits," the bartender said then turned and left.

Joel just grinned. "Hell, Skeeter, after you get a couple shots down you won't even pay no nevermind to paying double price for drinks! Makes me wonder how much the girls charge?" He looked around, hopeful.

By nightfall they found out everything in this northern town was at least double or triple the price of what they were used to paying. A sleeping cot in a large room full of snoring drunks cost a dollar a night. A decent room cost up to five dollars a night as opposed to fifty cents to two dollars, depending on the quality, in Texas or Kansas. When it came to food, fifty cents would buy a bowl of gruel or greasy stew, while a decent meal of meat, potatoes and bread cost one to two dollars, whereas twenty-five cents to fifty cents was common for fare in cattle towns. It cost a dollar a day just to feed and house a horse. The high prices were merely the cause of high demand by the growing crowd of wide-eyed strangers coming to a gold rush. At times during the day or night a thousand men or more crowded the streets and business establishments. It was indeed a carnival atmosphere to merely sit and watch the activities up and down the street. Freighters coming in to deliver goods and getting their wagon stuck in the muck on the street while teetotalers pointed and laughed, others would rush out to lend a hand to the stranded wagon. Hammers banged in the clear morning air as carpenters worked at a frenzied pace in getting a new building erected, while nearby in the street, donkeys brayed and freighters urged on their teams with cussing commands.

This was Deadwood.

CHAPTER 6

A whole month passed while the four Texas men attempted to blend into the town while making at least one visit to the more than fifty saloons with seemingly a new one opening daily. It didn't take long for them to figure out which places to avoid and they tended to stick with The High Grade as their choice of saloons. The High Grade offered twenty-cent beer, a free lunch assortment of meat and cheeses, round the clock card games, and saloon girls who were friendly. It was the kind of saloon the Texas cowboys were used to and expected.

After a time, the partying and laying out more cash than they had imagined, it was Willie who sought to change things when he came into the saloon and settled at a table with the others. "I think I found a way we can make some money instead of giving it all to the merchants and dealers."

Joel set his half full whiskey glass down. "What do you have in mind, Willie?"

"I ran across a man last night who wants to sell his quartz mine," Willie said.

"If it's any good why does he want to sell it?" Skeeter smirked.

Willie poured himself a drink from a rye bottle

sitting in the middle of the table. "He's sick, least he said he was. He just wants enough to get himself back to Louisiana before he dies."

"How much is he asking for it?" Joel asked.

"He said four hundred dollars would buy everything, the claim with a cabin tent and digging tools included.

"It's not too far from here, a couple miles," Willie continued. "It sounded pretty good and I thought, if everyone agreed, then we could take a look and give it a try. I, for one, am tired of these prices in town. It wouldn't cost anything to live out at the mine excepting the grub, of course."

Willie, Skeeter, Joel, and Sam rode out to the mine and liked what they saw. They pooled four hundred dollars and bought the claim as equal partners. The thought of making a rich strike was on each man's mind when they moved into the former owner's campsite which consisted of a ten by sixteen cabin tent. It had log walls four feet high then a canvas tent completed the top half of the walls and roof of the cabin with a tin stove inside. There was even a small corral and brush covered lean-to for the horses.

The four men spent two weeks of sloshing in ice cold creek water and made a half-hearted attempt to make the mine pay and earn an honest living. By now it was late into the fall. As the days grew shorter, wind funneling from the north had a definite chill to it. Evenings were spent huddled around a table and chairs made of tree limbs, near the cabin stove while drinking whiskey and playing cards.

It didn't take Joel long to figure that the mine held little gold, and that he wasn't cut out for the back-breaking labor a profitable mine required. The mine had quartz rock, but little of it was gold bearing and they had no equipment to bust out of the rock what little gold flecks that could be seen by the naked eye. Joel had lost interest in squatting and working a pan in the icy water of the creek that fronted the claim.

Willie and Skeeter had turned in for the night and were both snoring while Sam and Joel still sat before the stove. Joel spoke, the words coming in a near whisper. "I believe this mining is for others to do. I'd just as soon take my chances on the turn of a card."

Sam nodded, then got to his feet and retrieved the whiskey jug and poured himself a cup full. "I don't think this mine is as good as we all thought it would be," he said. "When I was back in Denton, I did some freight hauling. I figure the owners of the company made good money at it. I know I never missed a payday and it seemed like we were always behind in the deliveries. Deadwood has got two, three times as many people living here and they all need stuff. All the freight that comes in to Deadwood has got to come from somewhere. We could go into town tomorrow and see about some freight hauling. We'd have to buy a wagon, but we already got horses that ain't doing anything but growing lazy. It would beat hell out of freezing our fingers in that icy creek."

Joel nodded. "I don't think that Willie and Skeeter are ready to give up on the mine just yet. Between the two of them, they panned out nearly half an ounce of gold today. They might get ten dollars for it. It isn't enough of a showing for me though, so freight hauling sounds right down my alley. I'll go with you in the morning."

Over a mid-morning meal, Joel told Willie and Skeeter of his and Sam's intention of seeing about doing some freight hauling. Willie was more than eager to get back to the panning in hopes of doubling yesterday's take. "Skeeter and I want to pan some more dirt out of that hole we were working yesterday, so we'll be right here when you get back."

It was Joel, the better salesman of the two, who was able to secure a haul from Cheyenne to Deadwood, a load of dry goods needed by Sikes Mercantile. Joel and Sam rode to Cheyenne and bought a wagon for a hundred dollars. It was a high price for a farm wagon, but the price included the traces, collars and singletrees, a complete outfit. Sam and Joel were able to get the goods loaded, which was mostly sacked flour and cornmeal. With winter weather at hand, a canvas tarp was purchased and wrapped around the load. That would have been sufficient in a simple snowstorm but what they encountered twenty miles from town was a deluge of heavy rainfall.

When they pulled the wagon to the back of Sikes' store and lifted the canvas, it was clear that despite the covering, water had gotten to the cargo. Fortunately, it was only the bottom layer of goods that was soaked. Sikes threw a fit, then shrewdly figured out that since some of the goods had been destroyed the freight bill was null and void. Sikes insisted that Joel and Sam owed him a hundred dollars against, he quickly calculated, inflated prices of the lost goods. When Sam and Joel began to walk away, Sikes indicated that he would be lodging a complaint to the authorities. Joel and Sam took their horses but left the half-unloaded wagon. They checked the horses into the livery and then headed for the saloon.

"He can have that damned wagon as far as I'm concerned," Joel said. "If I'd have known that Sikes was such an asshole, I'd of took that load of stuff and sold it to someone else."

Sam laid a coin on the bar to pay for two beers. "Yeah, he can keep the wagon, we're out of the freighting business, anyway."

It was a sorrowful meeting with Willie and Skeeter back in the mining camp when Sam announced the failure. Willie told of his and

Skeeter's findings of not double the amount of gold but less than half of what they had expected the last few days. The mine was so poor it was considered a failure and now Sam and Joel were unable to do a simple thing like freighting some goods. It was too much to bear. They were all depressed and sought solace in the contents of a bottle of rye whiskey. Thereafter, the four rogues fell into slovenly ways, staying up until drunkenness forced them to retire in the wee hours of mornings, leaving them dead to the world until well into the afternoon.

Joel and Sam had given up on the mining altogether but kept the camp as a place to sleep out of the weather. Willie and Skeeter still maintained there was gold to be found at the site and spent most of their time at the camp. The horses were given portions of sacked grain from town so they didn't have to pay to board the animals. By early evening, Sam and Joel would return to the comforts of a saloon for a beer or so, which inevitably led to whiskey drinking and gambling all over again. The ideas for the making of legitimate money seemed exhausted and nothing more was mentioned of it.

Joel's and Sam's background of being some-what experienced gamblers with the ability to pull off a cheat from time to time back in the cow towns of Texas and Kansas, was an option that could no longer be risked in Deadwood, although they had tried. But the professional gamblers in the town were too sharp and the stakes too high, and inevitably Joel and Sam had no choice but to leave the games, sadder but wiser men.

A long dry spell followed, and there was no regard for conservation when it came to cash in their jeans. So the entire cold winter was spent in mindlessly squandering the herd money they had previously stolen.

One night, in the High Grade Saloon, Joel introduced Sam, Willie and Skeeter to two men who sat sipping from beer mugs at a table next to theirs. One man, Jack Davis, was known by Joel from back in Texas. The other man's name was Tom Nixon, and he was new to everyone. Both men appeared to have led tough lives. They were tall and lean of frame with a certain hunger in their eyes. Davis and Nixon were also cattle drovers who had finished a drive to a northern destination, then had been drawn to the goldfields with illusions of quick riches. The two had acquired a placer mining claim as well, with similar results to Joel and his group's mine. The harsh reality of gut-busting work in brutally cold weather, for little more than eating money, had taken a toll on the men. Jack indicated that he and Nixon would be going back to Texas, if things did not improve at the mine. A short time later Davis and Nixon called it a night and left the saloon, presumably to return to their claim.

• • •

It was a cold spring morning, and the men were lounging in the cabin over the midday meal when Willie suddenly spoke up. "Skeeter and I are pretty tired of trying to make this mine pay. The gold just ain't there!" He turned to Joel. "You figure we'll be here much longer?"

Joel took a deep breath then sipped his coffee before giving an answer. "I believe this high living has caught up to us, and those damned card dealers in the saloons won't let a man win a decent pot. The way the weather has been, with six inches of snow still on the ground, I reckon we're not going anyplace real soon. I'm thinkin' we better keep what money we got in our pockets until it warms up some. Then we'll head south."

Sam wasn't particularly worried. He'd been busted before and had come out of it. Failing at mining, freighting and gambling had put all of them into the worst possible position, trying to overcome in a town where gold was paramount. All they could do now was to try and survive Deadwood, a place where a man could get his throat slit for half a dollar in broad daylight, resulting in an unmarked and shallow grave in the rapidly growing cemetery at the far edge of town.

In spite of the dismal thoughts, Sam was still confident Joel would come up with something just as he had twice before.

With most of the money gone, no job to fall back on and things being tight, Sam simply fell back into doing what came to hand: something he hadn't done for a long time, outright stealing. Snitching a sausage and a few crackers at the mercantile, a scoop of grain for his horse when the stableman wasn't looking. He even picked a wallet from a coat hung on a rack at the hotel restaurant and was rewarded with twelve dollars. Nights proved to be a good time to wander the shadows for any drunks who fell to the ground. Lifting a watch or pocket change was usually all he could expect, using a quick hand under the guise of helping the liquor-sodden man to his feet. Every theft emboldened him to take even bigger chances for scant payoffs.

Finally, one bright spring morning, Joel finished his meal and then sat back in the rickety cabin chair. "I figure it's time we took out of here," he declared. No argument was forthcoming from any of his three companions. They rose as one and began their preparations, sure and certain Joel—like the biblical patriarch Moses—would soon be leading them to the Promised Land.

It was past noon before they had packed their clothes and camp gear on the horses and then rode away from the claim without looking back. They had ridden only a few miles when the creaking noise of the stage headed to Deadwood could be heard coming along the road a short distance ahead. Joel reined his horse to a halt then began pulling a bandanna up to mask his nose and jaws. "Let's just wait until that stage catches up to us and we'll see what they got for gold and cash."

Sam, Skeeter and Willie didn't seem at all surprised by Joel's sudden action and they immediately began obediently donning masks of their own without the least bit of reluctance. All four men had all been softened by lavish living and were now hardened by their circumstance, none of them strangers to stealing. They were broke and needed a stake, even if it meant robbing the stage.

Sam had to admit that his heart began to thud when he pulled that mask over his face and drew his six-gun. All the thieving he'd done in the past was secretive and away from anyone's view, but this was all new. Sam didn't dwell on the idea that the taking what you wanted by force was that wrong or immoral, and it excited him. He wasn't aware of how much so until he realized his gun hand was shaking as he pointed it toward the coach.

The four horsemen blocked the road with six-guns drawn, and the stage driver immediately pulled the team to a halt. A quick search by Joel and Skeeter revealed no strong box full of gold and there was only one male passenger. Between the two, they took nine dollars total, only to endure a severe tongue lashing from the driver. "You sorry sons a bitches need to get some work!" he cursed sourly as he lashed the team forward.

After the stage left, Joel bemoaned their bad luck. "Damn! I thought all stages carried a strongbox with a little something in it. But this coach didn't even carry a box! And that passenger was as bad off as we are with next to nothing in his pockets." He parceled out the loot, keeping the odd dollar for himself. "What the hell," he grinned. "Maybe the next one will be better!"

A few days later, they were some ten miles from Deadwood when the stage from Cheyenne came lumbering up the roadway. When ordered to halt, the driver tried to stop the team, but in the excitement of the confrontation the team of horses spooked and lurched forward. The move startled both Skeeter and his horse, his reflexes causing him to pull the trigger. His six-gun fired, the bullet hitting the driver in the chest, and the stage team bolted away. The four bandits, unnerved by the shooting, didn't give chase. None had considered that anyone would get hurt.

"It was an accident!" Skeeter wailed. "I didn't shoot him on purpose! My damned horse shied and jumped, causing me to pull the trigger!"

The injured driver was able to get the stage to town before he died from his wound. Deadwood's citizens were outraged at the shooting. A reward of five hundred dollars was quickly offered for the bandits, dead or alive.

The gang of four should have figured it was time to make tracks from the entire area. Instead, being rootless, they roamed at will, looking for easy pickings on their casual way to nowhere. They didn't plan out any future robberies but were intent on making robbery pay. They rode a roundabout route that circled Deadwood, ten to fifteen miles distant, paying close attention to well-traveled roads until crossing paths with some unlucky traveler.

They rode north about sixteen miles to Crook City, another mining camp town. It wasn't much of a town, just a scattering of frame houses and log cabins in the bottom of a draw. There were, however, a hotel, restaurant and two saloons open for business. It wasn't anything like the carnival atmosphere of Deadwood and the establishments didn't charge the high prices that Deadwood demanded. The closest thing to law enforcement was the axe handles that saloon bartenders kept near to hand. Sam, Joel, Skeeter and Willie settled in for two days before leaving.

In the days that followed, the four brazenly held up any travelers they came upon, and took any valuables found. They stuck up two freight haulers and three stages, gaining a little over one hundred dollars for their skullduggery before finally slipping further south into Nebraska Territory.

The likelihood of some sort of gunplay from one of their hold-up victims was ever present and it caused Sam a bit of concern. He wasn't worried of his own safety, he never thought of death, but he had no intention of deliberately shooting anyone and none of his fellow bandits had exhibited that they would either. One man had already been accidently shot and with all the robberies they had done, there was a good chance that a posse might be looking for them right now. He didn't say anything to the others but he was glad to be putting Deadwood and the Black Hills behind them.

One night, just at dusk, the four men made a camp out of sight in a little hole of a canyon. Sam busied himself caring for the horses while Skeeter gathered firewood and Willie prepared the coffee. Joel had climbed to a vantage point to see if they had picked up any followers. There was a sudden panic when Joel yelled to them, "Riders coming!"

The three in camp dropped whatever they were doing and grabbed their rifles, jacking shells into the chambers. They turned to Joel for more news, surprised when Joel stood and began waving his hat. That certainly wasn't the action of anyone looking to dodge the law. Before long two riders appeared next to Joel, who had returned his hat to his head and then reached out and shook one of the men's hands. He pointed to the camp and then motioned for the men to follow him. Sam and the others recognized the two men whom they had previously met in the Deadwood saloon as Tom Nixon and Jack Davis. Nixon had the carcass of a young doe deer tied to the back of his saddle.

Later, when all six men were lounging around the campfire still licking their fingers from the venison feast and sipping whiskey-laced coffee, Joel inquired, "You boys been doing any good since leaving Deadwood?"

Nixon smiled. "Things have been kinda tight. We tried to hold up a stage two days ago but the driver cussed us out and said four others had already held him up that morning. Was that you?"

Joel grinned, then answered casually, "Most likely. We hit everyone we came across. There wasn't much to be had in none of them."

Joel dumped the remnants of his coffee cup then stood to address the contingent of men who were huddled around the flickering fire, strengthened by a bit of wind. "We've been out here holding up coaches and travelers for chicken feed but there's bigger game just waiting to be taken." Sam and the others were still seated on their butts, listening quietly, wondering what scheme Joel had cooked up now.

"What I'm talking about is a train," Joel went on. "Others have been holding up trains for hell, ten, twelve years or so. I think it was the Reno brothers that made a big haul over in Indiana back in '66."

Sam, as a boy, had heard many exciting stories about the Reno brothers' deeds when he had lived with his uncle. The Reno brothers lived in Seymour, Indiana, only about forty miles from his uncle's farm.

Joel plunged on, "I heard they got ninety thousand, but that could just be a story. But every train has an express car that has a safe. It's called a 'way safe,' used for storing passenger valuables and maybe even a payroll. And then there's the passengers themselves and lots of 'em. Hell, most are well heeled, otherwise they wouldn't be using the train. Poor folks are the ones who ride wagons or horses."

Tom Nixon stood to lend his support to Joel's efforts in convincing the others. "I heard of trains being held up during the War. A lot of booty was taken that way, by both sides."

Joel cut in, "Anyone of you ever take part in such?" Everyone there shook their heads side to side, indicating no, while glancing left and right to see if anyone admitted that they had.

Eyes narrowing, Joel looked around. "With enough men, I figure we could take one. Once we make the hit, it would take only one or two men to keep the engineer in line and the train from moving. Two would hit the express car while others keep watch. After we're done with the express car we can see what the passengers have in their pockets."

"How do we get the train to stop?" Jack Davis asked.

Joel considered the man's words. "That's a fair question. We could barricade the track and they'd have to stop the train, but that puts anyone onboard with a shooting iron on the alert and ready to take pot shots at us. I prefer to work in the dark, when those inside the lit up coaches can't see what's going on outside. Trains run on steam, and they have to make water stops on a regular basis to replenish the water, otherwise the boilers would blow up. If we studied the route and found the water towers, it'd be just a matter of waiting until the train comes by."

"That sounds good to me," Willie piped up. "To hell with the goldfields up North and droving them damned Texas cattle! I've had enough. If it takes robbing a train to get me the hell out of here and back to the farm in Missouri, then I'm ready to go and the sooner the better."

Apparently everyone else was ready as well. Skeeter and Jack Davis tried to ask Joel questions at the same time. "Where do you plan on hitting the train?" Skeeter was quick to get in while Davis merely asked, "When can we do it?"

Joel showed his patience by answering each question as it was asked. "We'll need to travel to the South Platte River. That's where the railroad tracks are. We follow along the tracks until we come to a likely water tower that's away from any town. Then it's a matter of waiting for the right train."

"How do you know which train is the right one?" Willie asked.

Joel was quick to answer. "Other than isolation and darkness there ain't too much more we can ask for except hoping there's plenty of loot. To make sure, I figure we ought to ride into Ogallala or some other town and nose around a bit. Maybe we can get a handle on the schedule and such."

Early in the morning a few days later, the six men walked their horses down the street of Ogallala, arousing little interest as hundreds of Texas cowhands came and went during the season. They stopped at a store and bought a few supplies. Joel had the store owner cut two yards of calico cloth from a bolt before they left.

Sam took it upon himself to go to the train station and see what he could learn of the next arriving train. "Tomorrow night late, there's one due in from San Francisco," the agent said. "It would cost six dollars for a ticket to Omaha." Sam thanked the man and muttered that he'd think on it, then left. He headed straight for where he knew Joel and the others were waiting.

Joel's face lit up like a candle when he got the news. A train from California—gold rich California—could be carrying a hell of a lot of money. "Let's get on down the track and see if we can locate a tower," he said.

Keeping the tracks in view, they headed west. After about twenty miles, they located a water tower and a small station. From a distance, they observed a man leaving the station to visit an outhouse and return. For want of more information they rode on. In the late afternoon the six men could see in the distance the town of Julesburg, Colorado, a sleepy farm town near the South Platte River. Ribbons of shiny steel rails ran east and west through town.

Joel sat on his horse as he spoke to the others. "There are enough of us that we have the look of a gang on the prowl, not a good thing right now. I figure Sam and I will go into town to see about the train schedule, and if that station we passed is the right one. Everybody else ought to find a camp spot out of sight until we can find out what's what. We'll be back in the morning."

Tom Nixon nodded. "We'll go back to that little creek we crossed about a mile ago." He watched as Joel and Sam turned their horses, and then signaled for the others to follow him as they headed in the opposite direction to set up camp.

When Joel and Sam checked their horses at a livery, Joel pointed to the railroad tracks and asked the hostler, "Does the train come through here often?"

"Twice a week," the man answered. "Next one's due in tomorrow night at ten."

"Does it make any other stops nearby?"

"Far as I know, it goes about twenty five miles up the line to the Big Springs for a water stop and then on east to Ogallala and beyond."

"And always on time, I'll bet," Joel grinned.

"I believe so," the man said.

"Know a good place to eat and drink?" Joel asked.

The man nodded his head toward the street. "Vern's Hotel has got everything you need."

A stubby man of middle years, slightly balding, spun a register around. "Just sign right here and I'll get your keys."

Each man paid a dollar for the room and took the keys offered then walked into the hotel restaurant and seated themselves. A matronly woman came to take their order, bringing the coffee pot with her. A short time later the woman brought their meals. Sam and Joel wolfed down beef steaks, potatoes, biscuits, and lots of coffee. Afterwards they walked into a small and subdued hotel saloon. They soon learned that there weren't any girls working the floor, no card dealers waiting to draw them into a game and no piano. The place wasn't anything like the cowtown saloons or even Deadwood's dens that were boiling with activity, smoke and noise.

Apparently folks came to this saloon just to get a drink after their day of labor. The saloon was as flaccid as the whole town. Sam and Joel retired to their rooms when the bartender began closing at 10 p.m. The few local patrons had all gone home.

The next morning at breakfast Sam said, "This place is too quiet for me, I'd go stir crazy before the week was out."

Joel sat back in his chair. "Yeah, I couldn't stand much of this either. Let's get a bottle and go find the others," he said softly.

They retrieved their horses, bought some smoking tobacco and a two dollar bottle at the mercantile, and then mounted and rode to their companions' camp.

Joel told everyone in the camp what he had learned from the stableman. "All we need to do is go back to the water tower and keep out of sight until the train comes by tonight."

Four hours later they could see the Big Springs tower in the distance. "That stationkeeper is most likely inside the building so let's stay a ways off and watch," Joel said. They found a hub of oak trees a few hundred yards away. "Let's camp here until it's time, but no fire. It's as good a place as any to wait."

"You figure it'll be worthwhile to take on that train?" Skeeter asked.

Joel wondered if Skeeter was getting cold feet. "It's gotta pay better than stagecoaches and freighters. Might have a good strongbox and there could be some passengers flush with cash and jewelry. All we have to do is get aboard the train and see."

Skeeter nodded but seemed nervous.

As they lounged around the little camp Joel outlined the plan. "Tom and Willie will get the drop on the engineer and fireman. Jack and Sam will take care of the express car. Skeeter and I will keep watch, then we'll hit the passengers." Joel pulled the calico cloth from his saddle bags and tore it into squares. "I bought this special so's we all got masks," he said as he pulled some strings from his piece.

Skeeter, getting excited, took one and tried it on. "They might start calling us the calico bandits!" he joshed.

At 10:15 the six men donned their new calico masks. The station house window showed dim lamp light spilling out when Joel and Skeeter walked through the front door with six-guns drawn. The keeper, a slim man in his sixties was surprised but gave no resistance. "What do you usually do when the train comes by?" Joel asked the man.

"I walk out and hold a red lantern as a beacon for them to stop," the man replied.

Joel cocked the hammer of his weapon and placed the barrel against the bone behind the stationmaster's left ear. "I hope you're telling me straight, old man. I wouldn't want to have to start shooting."

The wide-eyed old timer nodded. "I won't give you any cause for shooting."

At 10:30 they could hear the train coming. Jack stepped outside and looped a rope around a nearby sagging telegraph wire, pulled it down and cut the line.

Hustling the station man toward the door, Joel issued his instructions. "Just walk out with that lantern and do as you usually do and you won't get hurt," he told the station man. "I'll be close by and watching."

It was 10:45 p.m. with a half-moon showing when the train came lumbering down the track, wheels squealing as it approached and ground to a halt. They all watched, listening to the puffs of steam as it escaped the pistons. Bright sparks, embedded in the heavy black smoke that poured from the smokestack, wafted ruby red against the nighttime sky before dropping onto the ground. The sparks glimmered for a moment or two in the darkness before going cold and fading into black oblivion.

The engine inched along to a precise spot near the tower just short of the station man's red lantern then halted. Sam and the others waited out of sight, in the dark, next to the building. Everything seemed to be going as planned.

When Willie and Tom came in from opposite

sides of the engine just as it came to a full stop, the engineer and fireman both stood erect and held their hands in the air. Willie instructed the two men to turn around. "Just keep lookin' straight ahead," he ordered. "And don't worry about your schedule. We won't be keepin' you long!"

Jack and Sam hurried down the side of the train to the express car's sliding door. Jack stood right in front of it. He pounded hard on thick planking. "Open up! This is a holdup!" The kerosene light that had flickered through the cracks around the portal abruptly disappeared, the squeal of metal against metal coming as the door slid open to a darkened interior and the loud bark of a six-gun from inside. Instinctively, Jack dropped into a crouch beside the car and then stuck his six-gun into the opening and fired three quick shots into the darkness.

Sam, who had been standing to the side of the door on Jack's right, began firing his six-gun as well. There was a grunt, and then a thud as whoever had been shooting at them fell to the floor of the car. Wary, Sam ducked down, but there were no further exchanges.

Jack stood looking in Sam's direction. "I think you got that bastard, I heard him hit the floor!"

From inside the car, there was the sound of coughing. "Don't shoot anymore," a voice begged. "I'm hit!"

"Throw your gun out!" Jack ordered. After a moment, a pistol clattered on the floor of the car and bounced out the door.

"Let's see what they're so damned protective of!" Jack said, climbing inside. Sam was right behind him. They found the wounded man sitting against the side wall illuminated by moonlight. "Is there a lantern in here?" Jack demanded.

"Over to your left," the man ground out.

Jack found the lantern and struck a lucifer to light it.

Sam stepped over to the downed man who was holding his right arm, blood oozing between his fingers. "Let me see," Sam said. He ripped the man's shirt sleeve to view a holed arm. "Give me your handkerchief." The man reached inside his pocket and produced one and Sam immediately tied it around the wounded arm. "You'll live. It didn't hit the bone. Who are you?"

The man's face betrayed his surprise at the question. "My name's Charlie Miller. I'm the express messenger."

Jack was busy looking at the large safe that was bolted to the floor. It was locked. He walked over to the bleeding man. "Need you to open that safe."

Charlie Miller looked up. "I can't open it. There's a timer set. It can't be opened until the time has expired, which is about when we reach Omaha."

Jack hit him in the jaw with his pistol. "Open it, damn you, or I'll shoot you again!"

Miller shook his head and spat blood from a split lip. "On my honor, I don't know the combination. I've got a paper here that says so." He attempted to reach his inside jacket pocket but Jack Davis batted his hand away, then reached and took out the paper himself.

Davis held the paper out to Sam. "What does it say?"

Unfortunately Sam had never learned to read or write either.

Jack became furious. "You better open it up, I'm telling you!" He screamed at Charlie and then hit the man another vicious blow with his fist.

Charlie Miller fell to the floor muttering, "I can't open it."

Alerted by Davis' yelling, Joel Collins swung up into the car to see what was happening. Grabbing the piece of paper Davis was waving in front of Collins' face, he read what was written and verified Miller's story. "Let him be, Jack, he can't open it." He shifted his gaze to Miller. "But you can open the way-safe, can't you?"

Miller nodded. Grimacing, he stood up and hobbled to the smaller safe and opened it. Inside there was four hundred fifty dollars in cash and a gold watch.

Sam found an axe attached to the back wall

of the car. He took it and pounded a few times against the combination lock on the big safe, but the axe blade was useless and he gave up.

Joel watched Charlie Miller while Sam and Jack ransacked the express car and eventually found three wooden boxes that were sealed in wax. Jack Davis took the axe and broke open one of the boxes. Twenty dollar gold pieces scattered across the floor. Each box had one thousand coins inside, twenty thousand dollars per box, sixty thousand total. Grinning, the three men carried the boxes from the express car.

Not wanting to miss the opportunity for an even bigger haul, Joel decided to stick with the original plan and to rob the passengers as well. "Skeeter and I will get the horses and keep watch. Sam, you and Jack go on in and finish the job. I'll go get Willie and Tom when we're ready to leave."

Jack entered the passenger compartment first. "Hold up your hands and keep still," he commanded as Sam followed close behind with an open sack. The men passengers stood grimly, the few ashen-faced women stood motionless. Sam stepped forward to each person in the line as they worked their way down the aisle, watching as the man or woman dropped their wallet or jewelry into the sack. The women would methodically open their purses and produce a few dollars or coins, and then reluctantly removed whatever jewelry they were wearing. When Sam was sure he had all that was to be had, he continued on.

When Sam came to an elderly man who had only one arm, he stopped. "Take your stuff back," he murmured, "we don't need your money. Sit down and keep still." The man complied and Sam stepped to the next person in line. It took only minutes to take all the money and jewelry that the passengers produced, although some people further down the line had in all likelihood managed to stash a ring or cash in a pocket or the bodice of a woman's dress.

The bandits were in too much of a hurry to search, question, or threaten. Sam exited the car while Jack held his six-gun on the wide-eyed passengers, then he too backed out the door and jumped to the ground.

The six rode hard away from the train for the next quarter hour before Joel had the others slow their horses to a walk in order to cool them down. When he brought his horse to a halt, he slid from the saddle, fished in his saddle bag, and brought out the bottle he'd bought at the store. He took a long swig and then handed it to Sam who stood nearby.

"That ol' boy in the car opened up on Jack as soon as he opened the door!" Sam said excitedly. "Jack and I both shot into the car. One of us hit the sucker! I'm surprised his shot didn't hit you,

Jack! You're mighty damned lucky, but we got him good though."

"Too bad we couldn't get that big safe open," Joel said, "but we made a good haul, a lot of cash."

"You think they'll be coming after us?" Sam asked.

Joel was quick to answer, "Yeah, I do, just as soon as that train makes it to town. They won't take lightly to us getting that gold. There's bound to be a posse coming right soon. I think we ought to ride north. We'll cross a few streams to throw them off, then we'll double back and go into Ogallala in the morning to see what kind of hornet's nest is stirred."

They rode north under the bright moon. Sam's mind whirled as they rode along. He had never felt guilty about stealing and he was still exhilarated from the robbery. He was not denying that robbery was now his chosen profession for the thrill it gave him. Sam enjoyed taking cash and property from others, using force to silence their objections, and lording over them while in complete control. He wondered how Joel could remain so calm. He also realized that every time the gang made a move it was because they were reacting to one of Joel's newfound schemes.

Sam hadn't planned to shoot that man in the express car. It had just happened and now there was nothing he could do to undo what was done, but at least the man would recover. Now that they had made a good haul, he had thoughts of going back to Texas but kept quiet as they rode along.

At about three a.m. Joel called a halt next to a tree-lined creek. "I'm ready for some coffee," he announced, "and we need to rest and so do the horses."

Sam began making a fire and Willie took care of the animals while Joel seated himself on a nearby log with the sack of booty taken from the way safe. Watching from a distance, he observed Joel counting out six equal stacks of cash.

"Comes to seventy-five apiece," Joel announced, "and there's a watch here, if anybody wants it."

Sam remained silent when he walked over and scooped up a stack of bills, as did Willie. All six men, tired from the robbery and the riding, were soon napping on the open ground.

As the first light of dawn on the eastern horizon began to show, Joel was up and bent over a skillet cooking some bacon when Sam and the others begun to stir. Quiet now, they dined on fried bread, bacon and coffee.

Joel finished the last of his bacon and spoke up. "I think we ought to stash this loot someplace and ride into Ogallala and check things out."

No one objected to the suggestion, and after cleaning up, they immediately saddled their horses.

When the town came in sight they located a spot protected by a grove of trees. The ground was moist and covered with knee-high prairie grass, and the terrain littered with an abundance of rocks both large and small. Dismounting, they found what appeared to be a collapsed cairn, a long abandoned boundary marker that had fallen into ruin. Joel determined it would make the ideal place to stash their loot.

Then, two at a time, the men leisurely rode into town. Paired off, they lounged around the saloons, feigning surprise as they heard the news about the robbery.

By mid-afternoon a good number of the men in Ogallala had ridden out to Big Springs to have a look at the scene of the holdup. Amos Leach, the owner of the store where Joel Collins and the others had bought their goods two days earlier, went along. In an area that had been used to hold the horses, Leach picked up a scrap of calico that had been torn from a larger piece. He recognized the cloth and remembered selling two yards of it to Joel Collins and rightly suspected the material was used as masks for the gang. He went on back to town but kept his finding of the cloth a secret.

Upon his return to town he learned of a ten thousand dollar reward being posted for the capture of the men who had robbed the Union Pacific Express at Big Springs. He remained mum and returned to his store to finish off the day.

Joel met up with all the bandits at The Big Chief Saloon. In a quiet corner of the saloon he addressed them. "I think you all found that the town folk are doing quite a bit of talk regarding the holdup, and now a ten thousand dollar reward has been posted by the railroad. I believe, though, that we have escaped suspicion. On toward dark we need to go get the loot and head out of this country before it's filled up and crawling with reward hunters. I heard the railroad has complained to the Army and they may send some soldiers out to scour the hills. So let's go over to the store and get some supplies before we take off."

Leach was on duty when the six men came into the store. He recognized Joel Collins from the time he had bought the calico cutting. "Have you heard about the big reward?" he asked.

Joel Collins was digging in his pockets for money to pay for his items. "I could sure use that ten thousand dollar reward, but somebody else will most likely get it. I've never been one to have such luck."

Leach was suspicious. He studied each man as they paid for their purchases and watched as the six of them went in different directions to gather their horses before leaving town. Closing up his store, he went and got his own horse. He waited until the last two men left and then followed at a discreet distance. When they stopped in a grove of trees just outside of town, he waited out of sight, silently watching. Ten minutes later the six men mounted and rode away.

Leach was able to follow from a distance until it was late in the night and the six men stopped to make camp. He was surprised at how careless they were leaving such a clear trail, and even more astounded when they failed to post a lookout. Creeping up just beyond the light of their campfire, he watched as Joel Collins divided up the loot, five hundred gold coins to each man plus cash and jewelry from a separate sack. He listened intently when Joel Collins began to speak.

Collins was on his feet beside the fire. "We need to split up. A six-man trail is too easy for the posse to dog. Since we've managed to escape suspicion, it would be better if we travel in pairs."

"Can I ride with you, Joel?" Skeeter was quick to ask before anyone else had the opportunity.

Joel smiled and nodded. "I plan on going back to Texas, Skeeter. If you want to ride with me, that would be fine. Hell, I might even go on down to San Antonia and square up with Henderson and Cranston," he chuckled.

Tom and Willie paired off and said that they were going to head toward Willie's home in Missouri. That left Sam and Jack Davis. Sam turned to face Jack. "I reckon to head south."

Jack nodded. "Sounds good to me. I've had enough of this northern country."

Sam threw the dregs of his coffee into the fire and then walked over to his horse. "Once we get into Kansas we can decide where to go from there."

The men came together for a final farewell and all shook hands. Then, pairing off and mounting their horses, they headed off in their chosen directions.

Leach had seen and heard enough. There was no way that he would confront any of the paired bandits, but figured he could sure enough notify the authorities in hopes of receiving a portion of the reward money for his efforts.

Thanks to Leach, by the end of the next day descriptions of the bandits had been sent out. Law enforcement officers in southern Nebraska and northwestern Kansas were informed by telegraph of the bandit's intended routes. Within a day, posses hungry for the ten thousand dollar reward posted by The Union Pacific Railroad were combing the alerted areas of Nebraska and Kansas.

Willie Jacobs and Tom Nixon headed east along the north shore of the Platte River, figuring to out-guess or dodge any posse they assumed would be looking for anyone passing into Kansas. They planned on going all the way to

Lincoln City and then it would be a short trip to the northwestern corner of Missouri.

Joel Collins and Skeeter Wilcox took a straight-away southern route hoping to get into Kansas and do more or less as Sam and Jack had prescribed, maybe blend into one of the cow-towns before traveling on.

CHAPTER 7

Eight days after the robbery, Joel Collins and Skeeter Wilcox came to a store at a crossroads called Buffalo Springs in Ellis County, Kansas, which was a few miles distance from Hays. They bought tobacco and some potatoes and coffee. While lounging outside the building, Joel was startled to see a reward poster tacked to the wall. It gave a description of himself, Sam Bass, and the other members of the gang. He ripped the poster off the wall, folded it and stuffed it in a pocket. He nudged Skeeter with an elbow. "Time for us to go."

A man who had been sitting in a chair in front of the building had watched as Joel Collins took the poster off the wall. When Joel and Skeeter mounted and left, the man stood and walked over to his horse. He rode a short distance outside town to a nearby camp where the Ellis County Sheriff, John Bardsley, was bivouacked with a detachment of ten soldiers.

Sam Bass and Jack Davis had taken a southeastern route toward Texas, hoping to pass through Kansas using familiar cowtowns as landmarks. Then it would simply be a matter of following old cow trails into Texas. The pressure of numerous posses crawling everywhere forced the pair to do some shrewd riding to elude them. On one occasion, they merely pulled their horses to a halt behind some squat black oak trees and sat watching as the posse rode right past them.

They soon learned to spend their days lying in the shade of tree-lined ravines where they could nap out of sight in thick brush. Travel was done in the dark of night which enabled them to spot the various campfires of their pursuers and easily avoid them. After a few nights' travel, Jack's horse began favoring a left rear hoof, perhaps having bruised the frog. Jack examined the hoof but couldn't find anything out of the ordinary. However, before long the horse began limping.

It was just after dawn when they came to an open field, possibly a pasture for cows or horses. Sam sniffed the air. "I smell wood smoke and coffee. Let's see if we can find where it's coming from."

"It might be a posse camp," Jack cautioned.

"We haven't seen any camps this far south all night," Sam assured. "This field has been worked so I figure there's a homestead somewhere nearby. Maybe we can get breakfast and see if they might have a horse that we could make a deal on."

In an open clearing they spotted a rough board cabin free of paint. Smoke curled from a rusty stove pipe situated on a sagging roof. It was a pinchpenny homestead, long on work and short on cash. The corral was pieced together with poles, some being wired together. The barn and other outbuildings were covered with salvaged lumber, possibly from a neighboring farm whose owner had given up.

A bare-headed, slender man wearing a patched shirt and loose bib overalls had a milk bucket in hand as he walked pigeon-toed across the yard on the balls of his feet as if his thighs were galled or he had a bad case of piles. The man didn't exhibit any signs of alarm when he became aware of the two strangers approaching, but merely stood still and watched as the men walked their horses up close to him.

"Morning," Sam offered cheerfully. The man nodded.

"We saw the smoke from the chimney and smelled the coffee. We've been out all night and are sort of lost. Don't mean to be a bother but we were wondering if you might allow two hungry men some morning coffee?" Sam inquired. "We've got money to pay," he added.

The man looked at the ground. "We ain't got much, but I suppose you could have a little of what we do have. Are you part of the posse that's been chasing after them train robbers?"

Sam decided to play along. "Yeah, we're like every other damned fool around, trying to figure out how to get in on that reward money. Why, with all the folks beating the bush, I believe it's almost like a gold rush." He removed his hat and gestured toward his companion. "I'm Joe Hayes and this is Mack Anderson."

"Alex Hardenson," the man responded. "There was a group of six came by yesterday, told us all about it. Said two of the robbers was caught and killed a couple days ago over near Buffalo Springs."

Sam sucked his wind in at the news but didn't want to show alarm. He knew if what the man said was true then it was a matter as to where the two were caught up with before he could surmise who it was. Joel and Skeeter were more or less traveling south and east the same as he and Jack were. Willie and Tom should be up north someplace and headed due east. "They got two of them, huh?" Sam asked trying to be as casual as he could. "Where's Buffalo Springs?"

"It would be southwest of here, might be forty, fifty miles by the way the crow flies. The deputy told me it was them all right. He said the sheriff and a group of soldiers rode right up on 'em, tried to arrest them then ended up shooting 'em from their saddles. They recovered part of the loot, a whole lot of brand new gold coins, hundreds of 'em, he said."

Sam was troubled by what he had just heard. If in fact this information held true it would mean that Joel and Skeeter had been caught up with and killed. He felt a moment of panic and thought about forgetting the coffee and riding like hell to get away to somewhere, anywhere that afforded safety. Jack grimaced then gave Sam a knowing look of apprehension that mirrored Sam's reaction to learning of their former partners' fates. After a moment Sam decided that running would be a rash move and that it was safe enough here to go ahead and get some coffee and talk about a horse.

"Is there anything that we can help you with before coffee?" Sam asked. "I can do that milking, if you want."

Hardenson nodded. "That would be a big help." He handed the bucket to Sam. "I'll just go in and tell Maggie to fix a little extra for breakfast."

When the man had stepped away, Jack asked, "Do you believe what that old man said about Joel and Skeeter?"

Sam shrugged. "I didn't like hearing what he said any better than you did, Jack, but yeah, I gotta believe it. He'd have no reason to say other than what he was told. I knew he wasn't joshing us when he said the soldiers found a lot of new gold coins. We will just have to keep our eyes open and be careful."

After Sam did the milking, he and Jack went inside the cabin. It was a cramped living area smelly with lamp oil and grease. The kitchen was part of the room on the left side. A table covered with a red and white checkered oilcloth sat in the middle of the room. Sam and Jack took seats in ladder back rickety chairs when the woman of the house smiled and pointed to the table. She was about fifty years old, presumably the same age as her man. She was skinny and frail-looking. Her skin had a jaundiced coloring. She had her graying hair pulled into a bun at the back of her head and wore a faded and threadbare cotton dress. She was cheerful, though, and smiled as she served the cornmeal mush and coffee. "That was nice of you to do that milking. Alex has been ailing of late," she said.

Sam nodded. "Glad we could help."

The woman poured coffee in earthen mugs then sat. "I hope you catch up to those robbers. It ain't right for some to go stealing what others have worked so hard for," she lamented. Alex Hardenson remained standing while eating and sipping coffee, further suggesting the man had some tender areas.

After breakfast Sam laid a five dollar gold piece on the table then he, Jack and Alex Hardenson stepped outside. Sam spotted a dusty and spider-covered buggy under an open lean-to roof and became inspired. "Do you use that buggy often?"

Hardenson glanced toward the hack. "Not like we used to. It's just me and Maggie here, we don't get out much."

"Would you be interested in selling it?" Sam asked.

Hardenson eyed him curiously. "I don't know." He studied the ground before speaking. "Maggie and I used to take a ride from time to time but she doesn't like to go just riding around without going on a visit to town." His brow furrowed as he worked the thing over in his mind. "What the heck would you have interest in that thing for? As you can see, it's been used a bit and been sitting for a while."

Sam answered right away. "Mack's horse has developed a limp. I don't think that it's anything serious and after a rest he ought to be good as new. We could get by using only one horse with a rig like this, otherwise we might be down to riding double or walking."

The old man continued to think on it. "That could be a problem being out here, we're a fer piece from anywhere. I reckon we could talk about it, though, that's if the price is right," he said.

Jack looked exasperated at the idea. "Hell, Joe, we'll have to give up the idea of any kind of overland travel except by following the roads. We'd have to just say the heck with it and go on home!"

Sam didn't flinch. "That's right. We're just two dumb farm boys heading home." Jack nodded his understanding and quieted.

Sam turned back to the farmer. "We'd trade you both our horses and the saddles for that buggy and your horse which is already trained to pull the rig. I wouldn't want you to think I was trying to get the best of you since I already told you that the one horse is limping a little. Fact is I'd give you an extra forty dollars just to sweeten the deal. I think Mack and I will give up on collecting that reward, we're both tired of all this and ready to go home."

Jack was driving the buggy while Sam sat beside him when they left. Jack was feeling peevish. "We should have looked at that horse before you made the deal. She looks pretty old and rundown. Hell, we'll be lucky to make it to the next farm, let alone Texas."

Sam thought of their current situation as a hand of cards. The odds against them were great but he'd faced big odds before and came out okay. Getting this buggy was like being dealt a wild card. It changed the game. Now if only they could play the hand out, win or lose they had to go on, there was no way to simply fold and walk away. He figured to ease Jack's mind a little. "Well, we ain't got time to be training a horse to buggy pulling and I figure those folks will take good care of our tired out horses. Besides I believe they could sorely use what little cash we gave them."

Jack was still argumentative. "We should've just made a deal on the horse instead of this buggy, now we might ride right into a trap with no way to escape!"

Sam gave a sigh and shook his head. "This little buggy is going to be our salvation. We have to play the hand that's dealt to us if someone comes to question us. The trick is to make them believe what they see, just a couple of down and out farm boys on their way home. Fact is, Jack, why don't you pull over as soon as we're out of Hardenson's sight?"

Jack pulled the horse to a halt behind a little knoll.

Sam stepped down. "Let's put the gold down flat on the bottom of the buggy and cover it up with our goods." They took the time to place the coins in neatly arranged rows on the very bottom of the buggy then carefully covered them with a burlap bag, their extra clothes, all the cooking gear and food stuff on top of that. Unless someone took everything apart, the gold was well hidden. Sam took his six-gun out of the holster and stuck the pistol in the top of his trousers then removed the belt and holster and rolled them into his slicker. Next he took his hat off and bent it out of shape to look more like a slouch hat and then placed it back on his head. "Now don't I look more like a farmer than a bandit?" he asked.

Jack nodded and did the same. "I hope I don't need any more than the six shots in this pistol," he declared. They didn't have a choice to do anything else to conceal their identity; ten days on the trail with unshaven faces and rumpled clothes had already done that for them. Satisfied that it was the best that could be done, they returned to the buggy seat.

Hardenson had said that the road due south led to Hays, nearby to where Joel and Skeeter had been caught. Sam and Jack figured to not take the chance of meeting already excited posse men and traveled a road that led southeast for the rest of the day. As the sun was dropping behind the western horizon, Sam started to pull up. "Let's camp and make a fire. I'm hungry."

Jack was quiet for a long moment. "You think we can risk a fire? There might be someone who sees the smoke and comes to check us out."

Sam shrugged. "I reckon I'll take my chances. We haven't seen anyone all day. If someone was to come by, we can't let them think that we're running scared. They'll judge us by what they see. If they figure we're trying to hide something then it tells them we're afraid and have a reason to be running. Next thing you know we'd be in the middle of a gunfight. It's up to us to convince anyone we meet that we have nothing to hide."

The Kansas flat country was lined by ravines flanked on both sides by red oak, white cedar, and short leaf pine. Thickets of dogwood lined hidden creeks. It was one of those thickets they maneuvered the buggy into and made their evening camp well away from and out of sight of the road and any prying eyes. Old Mabel, the mare, seemed content to munch the sweet grass next to the creek. Jack rubbed her down and reassessed her condition. "I reckon she's in pretty fair shape."

They did keep their campfire low and the night proved uneventful as no one came around.

The next morning as the grey light of dawn began on the eastern horizon Jack blinked awake and sat up, stretched and yawned and rubbed a hand across his stubble. He shoved the blanket aside and stood up. *At least they were alive and they hadn't been caught.*

For now.

Thoughtful, Jack stared up at the morning sky and wondered if a posse would catch up to them today, if he would still be alive at sunset. He pushed the notion out of his head. He couldn't afford to dwell on thoughts of death, or the news Joel and Skeeter were now cold and probably already in the ground. Mourning was something he would have to do later, after he and Sam were far away from the trouble and somewhere safe.

Levering himself up from the ground, he made up his mind to concentrate on the task at hand and the day ahead of him.

Jack was squatting by the fire stirring some frying bacon by the time Sam was finished with morning ablutions. "Morning, Sam," he greeted. "Coffee's done."

"Good morning to you, Jack!" Sam smiled. "I slept pretty sound. How did you do?"

Jack shrugged a shoulder. "Off and on. I'll feel better once we can get some miles behind us."

Sam took a tin coffee cup and filled it, then quickly set it down as the heat of the coffee radiated through the cup and made it too hot to hold with a bare hand. He took his bandana in his hand to hold the cup and began to blow into the liquid before cautiously sipping.

Sam could feel the uneasiness of his partner. "We're going to make it, Jack," he soothed. "Hell, just getting up in the morning under these circumstances is a gamble." He attempted to change the subject. "I figure we did better than twenty miles yesterday, not bad for that old mare. I hope she can do that and more today."

The sun had brightened to a clear morning as the two men ate their breakfast. A blue jay squawked nearby. Jack threw a piece of fried bread toward it. The bird bounced over, grabbed the morsel in its beak and flew away. After breakfast Sam cleaned the tin plates, skillet and cups with sand and creek water while Jack put the rigging onto Mabel.

They met no one on the road until mid-afternoon when a freight wagon pulled by a six mule team came lumbering toward them. The driver pulled his team to a halt as the buggy approached then stopped beside the wagon. "Howdy," the barrel-chested man said, "you're the only souls I've seen all day. It gets kind of tiresome to just talk to these mules. You boys look like you're on your way from somewhere."

"That's a fact," Sam offered, "we're on our way home from summer work. Where are you headed, mister?"

The man took out a rag and wiped his face. "I come from Salina. I got a whole load of goods for a fellow named Jewett that has a place, oh fifty miles or so north of Plainville. I expect to be on the road for a few days yet."

"Have you heard anything about some train robbers that half the country's looking for?" Sam asked.

The man nodded. "I ran across some soldiers yesterday, they asked the same thing. They didn't seem to know who they were after. They were just looking over anyone that they came across. I suppose in due time they'll catch whoever it is they're after."

The talk went on for ten minutes before both parties decided to travel on, each having learned little to nothing about the other.

Late that day Mabel was beginning to balk, showing that she was tired and wanted to rest, forcing Jack to snap the reins to keep her going. Sam and Jack began searching for another campsite when they both saw movement up ahead. It was a group of riders coming up the road two abreast. When he saw the soldiers approaching, Sam could feel the short hair bristling on his nape. Excitement mixed with fear. It thrilled him and troubled him at the same time. Riding straight at trouble offered the greatest cure for anything hum-drum.

Jack was troubled by what he saw and Sam could see him visibly stiffen on the seat. Sam was seasoned to remain cool under pressure, more likely to consider risks before lashing out to make a move that couldn't be reversed. He wasn't sure about Jack's demeanor.

"Steady on," Sam assured, "don't make any sudden moves, Jack, and let me do the talking."

When the column of twelve soldiers spread out and came to a halt in front of the buggy, Jack pulled Mabel to stand idle also. A young officer sitting tall in his saddle walked his horse forward. The stone-faced man took one look at Sam and Jack and seemingly discounted any cause for alarm. "Have you two seen six men on horseback while on your travels?"

Both Jack and Sam shook their heads side to side. "No, sir, we have not. We've been on the road all day," Sam said. "Should we be wary and concerned?"

"What are you fellas doing out here? Where did you come from?" the officer inquired.

"We've come from Uncle Alex Hardenson's place up near Plainville. Aunt Maggie sent us a letter said he was doing poorly and we went up to get in the hay and help out. He's doing better now so we're just on our way back home. Right now we're just looking for a place to camp for the night."

The man looked over toward a clump of red oak trees then looked back to Sam. "We're getting ready to make camp ourselves. This looks like as good a place as any. You men are welcome to join us nearby."

Sam nodded. "We'll do that." Jack stiffened further.

Jack pulled the buggy off the road a little ways away from where the soldiers began to strip the saddles from their horses and hobble them. Before long the soldiers had their campfire going while Sam made a smaller fire thirty feet away from the soldier camp and near the buggy while Jack attended to Mabel.

A sergeant walked over to Sam. "Lieutenant Barnes said to offer for you men to share a meal with us but all we got is beans, cornbread and coffee."

"Thanks, sergeant," Sam said. "We got beans and bread as well but we'll take you up on that coffee offer. We don't have a pot, just a can we boil water and grounds in."

Sam and Jack walked over to the soldier camp

with coffee cups in hand. The lieutenant said to a nearby corporal, "Perkins, go ahead and pour these men some coffee."

"Thanks," Sam said. "I'm Joe Hardenson and this is Mack Anderson. We're cousins."

"I'm Lieutenant Barnes. We've been dispatched to locate and detain some men who robbed a train up in the Nebraska Territory and are known to be heading into Kansas. So we stop everyone we come to."

"Oh, you'd have to do that, Lieutenant, we understand. I'd say that we're mighty lucky you come across us and advised us about those robbers. Come tomorrow, we'll sure be on the lookout! Can't be too careful, I reckon." Sam tried in earnest to sound sincere and figured to steer the conversation away from any reference to trains and robbers. "Now, how far you figure to travel before you return to the post where you're stationed?"

The lieutenant frowned. "The distance doesn't matter. I was ordered to take a detachment of men and spend two weeks looking before returning. We've been out for five days now, but I believe that we're too far south. I figure to cut north in the morning."

The evening was spent talking to various members of the group about such things as card games, women, and horses. Neither the lieutenant nor any of the soldiers questioned Sam or Jack any further. They had completely believed the story Sam had given them. Apparently Lieutenant Barnes and his men had been dispatched to patrol duty prior to the killings of Joel and Skeeter, and were unaware that the two men were dead.

The next morning, Sam and Jack shared coffee again before the group of soldiers headed north.

Jack swung the buggy onto the road facing a bright sunshine. "We're headed due east, Sam. When do we cut south?"

"If we head south now we would come to Ellsworth," Sam reasoned. "I think we ought to travel further east before we turn south and avoid any big settlements. Any lawman worth his salt is going to be on the lookout."

"So be it," Jack said.

It was three more days of travel before they came to a farm a few miles west of Junction City, Kansas. Jack stopped the buggy while Sam walked over to talk to a man in a field. When Sam returned to the buggy, he looked thoughtful. "That fella said there was a road running south from Junction City that goes right into Newton and Wichita. Then it's a straight shot south to Texas."

"You think we can trade this buggy off for some horses in one of those towns?" Jack asked.

Sam considered the question. "I think we'd be better off to bypass both places and do any horse trading a little closer to the Territory. I believe there's plenty of law in all these towns. We'll start looking as soon as we get further south."

They traveled six more days on their slow plod before coming to the outskirts of Caldwell just on the edge of the Indian Territories. Fortunately for them there was a string of three freight wagons heading into town. Jack pulled the buggy right in behind them and followed. Sam slipped to the bed of the buggy and carefully put the gold coins into two saddle bags then stuffed clothes over them. He put five coins in his pocket and handed five to Jack.

By the time Sam completed his chore, Jack had directed Mabel to a livery on the northern edge of the town. He drove the buggy right into the open barn. The owner of the livery didn't seem too interested in the buggy or the worn mare for trade until Sam produced three twenty dollar gold pieces. "That'll get you the one horse and a saddle. A second horse is fifty dollars. Those are good horses, too. I bought them off an outfit that was headed back to Texas. I don't have another decent saddle but you might try ole Luther over at the Side Trail Saloon, sometimes he takes 'em in on a liquor bill."

Jack paid the fifty dollars for a second sorrel cow pony.

"We'll be back to get the horses in the morning," Sam said. Then he and Jack walked out of the livery carrying the saddle bags and their long guns.

Sam gestured toward the hotel. "Let's get a room and get cleaned up," he suggested.

Once inside the establishment, they asked for and got one room with two bunks. When they reached the room, Sam set his saddle bag and rifle on the bed. "One of us needs to stay with the saddle bags while the other gets his bath and such." He grinned across at his partner. "You can go first if you want, Jack."

After both men were shaved and bathed, they changed into clean clothes. Sam moved his rifle and made himself comfortable on the bed, sinking into the two pillows he had stuffed behind his head.

"You think it's safe enough to leave the bags and go get some food and drink?" Jack asked.

Sam shook his head. "I don't have any trust for folks and places I'm new to. I believe that I'll spend the night right here in this room. It sure as hell beats trail camping. Why don't you go eat first, Jack? I'd like it though if you would bring me a bottle beforehand. Then when you come back after your meal, I'll go eat."

Jack left and a short time later brought a bottle of rye whiskey he had purchased at a nearby store then slipped out the door again. Sam contentedly drank from the bottle while he waited.

When Jack returned, he sat down on his own

bunk and began pulling off his boots. "Pretty good vittles at that little café. Sally's, I think it's called. It's only two doors down. I didn't go to the saloon yet, if you go after your meal, you might ask about that saddle."

Sam nodded and then left. No one seemed to notice the oddity of two men who traveled together yet dined alone.

CHAPTER 8

The next morning the two went to the livery and claimed their horses. Sam had paid fifteen dollars for the saddle from the bartender at the Side Trail Saloon. They saddled the horses, adjusted stirrups to fit and loaded their saddle bags onto the animals. Afterwards they walked the horses to a hitch rack directly in front of Sally's Café then went inside for a window seat and had breakfast. Afterwards they made a trip to the mercantile and replenished their supplies for trail camping. By the time they had bought coffee, bread, potatoes, bacon, some canned goods, smoking tobacco and a coffee pot they had two gunny sacks full of goods. They saw a man with a badge across the street while they were loading the sacks onto the horses but he paid them no mind as they looked just like all the other cowboys that came and went.

It was mid-morning by the time they left town heading into the Indian Territories. Even by taking a directly southern route they had a two hundred fifty mile trip before reaching Texas.

The journey was uneventful, ten days in the making. By taking a slightly east by south direction, they veered away from the northbound cattle trails and purposely came to Denison,

125

Texas in late October. Denison was just across the Red River from The Indian Territories. The town came into being in 1872 when the Missouri, Kansas and Texas railroad, commonly called the KATY, crossed over the Red River and established Denison as a railhead for receiving cattle for eastern markets.

The railroad's competitive move made it easy for Texas cattle owners to load their animals in Denison, saving the time and expense of having to travel all the way to the more distant loading points in Abilene, Wichita, Ellsworth and Dodge City, Kansas. Price dictated where the owners sent their cattle, so many still elected to go the distance to Kansas for a more favorable return.

Sam had been here before, three years earlier when he had struck out on his own as a race horse owner. He had left disheartened and almost broke after losing a good portion of his money on a race when Jenny had been bested by a big stallion. When Sam thought on his last visit here, it seemed to have been a millennium ago. Things were different now, he wouldn't be betting on a horse race and he had money in his pocket.

Sam and Jack sat on their horses looking across the river at the cluster of buildings.

"Have you been here before?" Sam asked.

Jack shook his head. "It's the first time for me."

"We can stay at the Crystal Palace Hotel," Sam

suggested. "It's the best in town, right on the main street. We can put our saddle bags in the hotel safe or leave them in the room, it should be safe enough either way because nobody knows what we are carrying. The hotel has a restaurant and saloon and a livery just for their guests. The next street over is Skiddy street, down in a ravine. You can drink, gamble, find a loose woman or get your throat cut if you're not watchful."

Jack laughed. "Hell, Sam, that ain't anything new! We've been trying to get ourselves killed off ever since Big Springs."

Sam smiled. "I think we outfoxed them, Jack. I don't believe that there's anyone on our trail so I figure to get cleaned up and start living a little. It's been a long dry spell for a drink of whiskey, a good cigar and a game of cards."

Three days later Sam was seeing Jack off at the depot. Jack had a train ticket to New Orleans. "I'm going to catch a freighter to South America, so I won't be leaving any tracks," he boasted. "Sam, are you sure you don't want to go with me? There's got to be some new opportunities down there."

Sam shook his head. "I reckon to go on down to Denton and look up some old friends and see what card I'm going to draw next."

The two men shook hands and then Jack stepped aboard the train and was soon gone.

It was November 1, 1877 when Sam rode into Denton with a thousand dollars in his pockets. He had stopped along the way from Denison and stashed the bulk of his gold coins in a cluster of rocks that was hidden by a thicket of cottonwoods. The place was a favored stop of Sam's where he would pull up and allow the team to water and rest when making deliveries for E&H Freighters a few years earlier. The pile of rocks hiding the loot, above the creek, blended with surrounding rocks and would not draw any undue attention.

Sam was jubilant when he rode to the open doors of Work's Livery.

Joseph Work, a brawny man of Swedish descent, stepped forward and studied Sam as he dismounted. When recognition came Joseph smiled broadly and stuck out his hand. "Didn't expect to see you, Sam, the last I heard about you was that you were off racing horses."

"I gave that up," Sam chuffed. "I turned to herding cattle for a while then went up to Dead-wood looking for gold."

"Did you do any good?" Joseph Work asked.

Sam nodded. "Yeah, I found some." He handed Joseph a five dollar gold piece. "The usual for my horse, scoop of grain and a rub down. I'll check with you in a day or so."

Joseph bobbed his head. "Good to see you, Sam."

The clerk at Martin's Hotel, a slim balding man, was someone Sam didn't know, a new arrival he guessed. "I'll take a room by the week," Sam declared. "Room Four, if it's available, I had that one last time." Actually it did not matter that much to Sam, it was just that he considered the number four to be a lucky number.

He paid with a twenty dollar gold piece.

The clerk fingered the coin. "This one looks like it was newly minted," he noted and then made change.

When Sam walked into the Red Horse Saloon, the place looked different to him, smaller and dingier than he remembered. The bartender, another new face, was busy with others so Sam walked over and sat at the same table where he had played cards many times before. Sitting there, Sam had a strange feeling come over him. Here he was back to where he had started. He wondered if this could be the end of the road or if it was the beginning of a new adventure? His thoughts dissipated when the bartender came to see to his wants then left and hurried back with a mug of beer.

Later Frank Jackson, Henderson Murphy, and Henry Underwood all straggled into the Red Horse. They and Sam sat sipping mugs of beer that Sam had bought. It was the closest thing to a homecoming Sam could expect. Though others in town all smiled and said they were happy to see him again, these men were his friends of long ago. Little did anyone know how starved Sam was for things such as a home, pals, a neighborhood to call his own, a family.

"You're looking good, Sam. Where in tarnation have you been?" Henderson Murphy asked. At forty-one years of age he was the old man of the group.

Sam lit a cigar, tipped his hat back and slouched in his chair. He would have to fabricate a story that these men and others would believe. "Well, as you know I left here with Jenny to try the race circuit. We did pretty good and won a number of races. Then one day she lamed in San Antonio. I put her to pasture and then being without a way to make a living, I signed on with an outfit to herd some cattle to Kansas, which we did. It took a whole summer to get those cattle to market. When the drive was done I partnered up with others and we went up to Deadwood and bought ourselves a gold mining claim. Let me tell you, it's colder than all get out up in that country. Too damned cold to camp out, hell, the coffee pot would freeze up overnight and pan washing for gold in creek water is something to remember. But the mine turned out to be a good one. We all made a bunch of money before the gold started to peter out so we decided to sell out and go our separate ways. So I thought I'd come on back down here and see how you boys were doing."

"Well, you sure as hell look prosperous," Frank Jackson said.

Sam smiled. "Yeah, me and my partners got real lucky." He lifted a hand to get the attention of the bartender for another round of drinks.

It did not take long for Sam to resume living the way he did in Denton three years earlier and with more enthusiasm and restlessness. He spent money freely buying drinks for anyone and everyone. The girls who circulated in the saloon magnetically hovered near for drinks and tips.

Three days had passed and it was early afternoon when Sheriff Egan strolled into the saloon and walked straight over to where Sam sat alone at a table while playing a hand of solitaire. When Egan took a seat, Sam laid his cards down and sat up straight.

"I heard you were in town. I thought maybe you'd come by the office and say hello," Egan said.

Sam stuck out his hand. "I've been aiming to do that, Dad."

Sheriff Egan shook hands with Sam then settled back in his chair. "I didn't figure you'd come back to this country but it looks to me like you've done okay for yourself." Egan knew that Sam was a natural rebel who resented having his life decided for him, that he was one who just had to get out and see what made the world go round. That told why Sam had left town

131

before, but didn't explain why he had come back.

"You want a drink, coffee or something?" Sam offered.

Egan shook his head.

Sam knew that the man wanted an explanation so he recited the not too accurate facts about the time spent racing, of retiring the mare then of trailing cattle to Kansas. He was careful to not mention the real owners of the cattle from San Antonio, just that it was a long trip. When he told of buying a mine in Deadwood, he didn't bother to give the names of his partners either.

"Sounds like a sure enough strike you fellas made," Egan commented.

Sam nodded. "It truly was a once in a lifetime find. I saw lots of others leave with little to show for their efforts."

Sheriff Egan was skeptical when he walked out of the Red Horse Saloon. He knew by Sam's short answers and averted eyes that the young man was fabricating his story as he went along. Part of Sam's story was true enough. He believed Sam no longer owned the race horse and he also believed Sam most likely did drover some cattle on a trail drive to Ellsworth, like he had said.

What he couldn't swallow easily was this claim to instant wealth, that Sam and others had bought a mining claim and then made an immediate discovery of riches. The previous owner had most likely gone over every inch of the claim before deciding the effort wasn't worth the return. Things like that *did* happen, but so did getting struck by a bolt of lightning, and just about as often.

As a lawman, it was his nature to be suspicious of unlikely activity. The Sam Bass he had known three years ago was a hard working young man who loved gambling and the comforts of fast living and drinking, whenever he had the money to do so. He never seemed to worry much about anything or do much planning for the future. He was unpredictable and also prone to be easily led. Egan figured Sam for a fool who would forsake any responsibility in his quest for money and adventure, evidenced by Sam's departure three years ago.

Egan wondered if whiskey or the gambling fever had gotten hold of Sam, if in his own weakness he had allowed himself to be led by others into doing something that was astray of the law. Time would tell, he figured.

It was the first day of winter, six weeks after Sam had arrived in Denton and late in the afternoon when Frank Jackson came into the Red Horse Saloon as usual. He stopped at the bar long enough to get a mug of beer then walked over to where Sam, Henderson Murphy and Henry Underwood were seated at their usual table gabbing about a saloon girl that Sam now favored since Mary Beth had moved on. Henry Underwood poked Murphy in the ribs with his elbow. "Who was that overgrazed cow you were sporting with last night, Sam?"

Sam smiled broadly. "She said her name was Cherry. She might be a little meaty, but I'll say one thing, she's sure a lot of fun!"

"A lot of woman there," Henry Underwood grinned.

"A lot a lovin'," Sam quipped.

Sam had been drinking his favorite brand of whiskey since before noon. He had begun drinking earlier in the day than usual and had drunk late into the night before with the new girl, Cherry. It wasn't like he was a stranger to drinking, of late he had grown used to it, unlike when he lived here before and would only drink more than one drink as he could afford it. One drink led to another and now he needed it.

Despite all the easy living the way he had wanted, Sam was becoming bored with the slow pace of things in Denton. He still hungered for excitement and had discovered the high he got from the exhilaration of the robberies and escapes was like a drug, and he was becoming addicted. He had also grown accustomed to rubbing shoulders with outcast men and women, the kind that infested the seedy saloons, dance halls, brothels, gambling joints and honkytonks on the lower side of towns. Places at night that with all the noise and smoke and dim lights excited the senses while at the same time repelling them. Darkened streets where one walked along with a hand on the butt of his six-gun, wary of shadows and trusting no one.

He recalled that on such occasions his heart pumped harder, but not from fright. He was committed to go where he chose in defiance to any or all who dared impede his path. But here, in Denton, he was trying to compel people to believe he was an upright man when he was actually as crooked as a dog's hind leg. It would be like saying a mule was a horse. No matter how you disguised it, though, it would still be a mule.

Sam's thoughts were interrupted when Frank asked, "Did you hear about the train robbery last night, up at Allen Station?"

Sam straightened in his chair, seemingly greatly surprised. "Someone robbed a train?"

"Yeah, I just heard Joe Martin, the telegraph operator, talking to the sheriff about it. He said that it was the first train robbery ever done in Texas."

Sam grinned. "Hell, someone beat me to it!"

"How do you figure that?" Henderson Murphy asked.

Sam's grin widened into a big smile. He'd had more than enough whiskey to prime his tongue, although it had certainly dulled his brain. "Let me tell you three a secret. You're all wondering

135

how I managed to make a strike in Deadwood. How much money I made and so on? Well, truth is, I didn't make the money in Deadwood. Fact is, the others and I starved ourselves out in that place, so we took to robbing stages and when that didn't pay much we decided to take on a train.

"I was part of the gang that held up that train at Big Springs, Nebraska that everyone's been talking about," he boasted, his voice a hoarse whisper. "We got sixty thousand in gold coins. My share was ten thousand the same as the others.

"Two of my partners were caught and killed, two others headed to Missouri. I don't know if they made it, I haven't heard one way or the other. But my traveling partner and I made it all the way back to Texas with our shares of the loot. He went on down to South America, as far as I know, and I came here."

The others were silent while Sam confessed the source of his wealth.

Henderson Murphy was slouched back in his chair, a beer mug in his right hand. He seemed to be studying the condensation on the side of the tankard, watching as it trailed down the glass to form wet rings on the table. "I guess I gotta believe you, Sam, but I don't know how you got away with it," he said.

Sam sipped his drink and then sat the glass down. "We were careful, watchful and took advantage of every situation. We changed our looks and were able to elude capture." He told of buying the buggy and riding it to freedom by looking and posing as dumb shit farm boys.

Frank Jackson, the youngest of the group, was bug eyed. "That's a hell of a tale, Sam! It sounds like it was a lot of fun outwitting those soldiers and even having coffee with 'em, right under their noses all the time. Wow! I wish I'd have been along. I'm damned tired of working all day and getting nothing but enough money for a few beers and some smokes to show for it."

Henry Underwood nodded. "Yeah, Denton doesn't offer much in the way of opportunity like that. You suppose you'll do it again, I mean when your dough starts to run low?"

Sam leaned back in his chair. "Even if I had thought about it someone else has gone and stirred things up. Now the railroad and the law will all be leery. I wonder if they got very much loot?"

Jackson shrugged. "I didn't hear how much, but so far they've gotten away. Hell, it doesn't matter. I'll bet there's plenty more to be had on other trains."

Sam nodded. "That's for sure. Are you interested in maybe taking one on?"

Jackson smiled. "Hell, yes, I'd like to!"

Henry Underwood spoke up, voicing his intention to join the others. "Count me in."

Henderson Murphy stood. "That's damned fool

talk, Sam. You might have snookered those looking for you up in Nebraska and Kansas, but just wait and see if those that robbed the Allen Station train don't end up getting caught. The law won't put up with train robbery in Texas."

Sam just smiled, feeling as though he had been challenged. "I guess we'll see. Anyway it's something to think on."

Murphy, seemingly disgusted, turned and walked away.

"Don't pay him any mind, Sam," Frank Jackson said. "He'll think on it and come back. He worries too much and thinks he knows it all because he's older than we are. But do you think we could really rob a train and get away like you did?"

Sam nodded. "Yeah, I do. The holding up of the train was easier than I thought it would be. It was staying out of the posse's way that caused some anxious moments. I wondered about things just like Henderson is doing. But Joel, our leader, he was the one that come up with the idea, said we wouldn't know if it could be done until we tried. Joel did all the planning but he ain't here no more. So I reckon I would have to be the one to study this thing out before a job could be done, that's if we ever decide to do it."

It was well into January by the time Henderson Murphy had decided to rejoin his beer drinking buddies. He came into the Red Horse Saloon, bought himself a mug of beer and then walked over to the table where Sam and Frank sat. Henry Underwood was away visiting relatives.

"I'd like to think that what you've been talking about can be done," Murphy said as he took a seat. "I won't stand in your way but I'm not of a mind to ride with you."

Frank grinned while giving Sam a knowing glance.

Sam took another long draw on his beer, wiping the foam away with the back of his hand. "We're going to need a base camp, a hideout when the law starts looking."

It was Murphy who spoke up after a long silence from the others. "There's a good spot in a canyon up near my place on Clear Creek. You can ride right past my place to get to it, we call it Cove Hollow. Nobody ever goes in there. The brush is too thick and the woods are full of rattlesnakes."

"Sounds like a good spot," Sam said. "I know some about that country north of here from my freighting days. I recall there being a lot of brushy hillsides. Can we ride out there and take a close look tomorrow?"

Henderson Murphy nodded in agreement.

The next morning they toured Cove Hollow and gave the spot Henderson had selected a seal of approval.

A few days later Sam and Frank Jackson sat at a table in the Red Horse Saloon. "It's time we get into action," Sam said. "When you get off work tomorrow, let's ride down to Dallas." Jackson didn't argue.

The next night Sam and Frank Jackson rode to the outskirts of Dallas. Less than three miles out they stopped a Dallas-bound stage, forced the passengers to disembark and demanded cash. They got forty-three dollars for their effort. It was reminiscent of the miserable showing that Sam, Joel and the others had netted from robbing the stages near Deadwood.

Sam was not to be deterred. Two nights later he and Jackson held up another Dallas-bound stage and took in four hundred dollars. The passengers had been slow in coming out of the stage and secreted away more valuables than they forked over. One man stuffed the bulk of his cash into a glove, which he left on the seat when he climbed out. The two bandits didn't do a search. Sam remembered his experiences at stage robbing and considered them minor episodes but he seemed satisfied that the robberies had been a good training ground for Frank Jackson and at least they got a little cash which elated Jackson to the point he quit his town job.

The next few days Sam and Frank worked on making their new hideout livable, pulling firewood out of a draw with their horses and cutting and dragging in new timber to be used as poles for a corral. They also spent time riding the surrounding hillsides searching out escape routes if flight became necessary. Night would find the pair back in Denton at the Red Horse Saloon.

After two weeks had passed, Sam was becoming anxious over Henry Underwood's absence from the group. Sam was ready to prove he could be as good a leader as Joel Collins had been and was ready to step up to a higher payoff. Robbing stages provided only a small return whereas the concept of robbing a train that held untold riches was heavy on his mind. *The results had been good in Big Springs,* he mused, *and there is no reason it won't work out here in Texas.*

Sam made his intentions known to Frank. "I think it's time to hit a train. I've got our water station picked out and I'm going down there tomorrow to look around. Henry's gone and we don't know when he'll be back, but I think we should get going on this. Trouble is, I just know we ought to have another man along and Henderson won't ride with us. I had a talk with Seaborn Barnes last night," he continued. "He's kind of rough when he gets in a fight but he might be a good one to ride with us."

Frank knew of Seaborn Barnes' reputation, he was not just rough, the man was known to be downright vicious when it came to brawling. But Frank didn't question Sam's decision of bringing

141

in the extra gun. A tough hombre might be good to have along in order to keep the train people calmed.

Lady luck's wheel of fortune had dealt a deadly card to Sam, a card that Sam was now forced to play. He recruited Seaborn Barnes.

On March 18, Sam, Frank Jackson and Seaborn Barnes rode their horses south to the water station Sam had picked out at Hutchins, south of Dallas. There was no station attendant, or a station for that matter, just a water tower.

No station attendant was needed. The engineer of the train knew when to slow down by the signs strung out along the track that measured his approach. Once positioned to receive the water, it usually took about ten minutes to fill the train's cavernous holding tanks before leaving.

It was a star-lit evening when the three watched as the engine approached, puffing balls of steam and cinders as it slowed.

Sam stepped right into his leadership role. "Frank, it'll be up to you to cover the engineer. Keep him from doing anything until we're done. Seaborn and I will hit the express car. I don't want to mess with the passengers, we don't have enough manpower to do that."

When the engine came to a stop, Sam trained his six-gun on one side of the engine cab while Frank Jackson entered from the other. After seeing that Frank had the engineer and fireman covered, Sam ran down the track to give Seaborn a hand with the express car. He placed a hand on the man's shoulder, then motioned Seaborn to move away from the sliding door. Sam then positioned himself on the other side of the door. He banged on the heavy planks with the barrel of his six-gun. "Open up in there!"

"What do you want?" an excited voice called out from inside the car.

"Open up or I'll build a fire under the car and burn you out!" Sam ordered.

"Just a minute," the voice said.

Seaborn didn't want to wait so he pumped three shots into the door. "Open up, damn you!" he roared.

As the door began to slide open, the express messenger, six-gun in hand, began shooting through the narrow opening. He didn't take the time to aim his shots but kept pulling the trigger until the gun was empty. Sam peeked around the corner of the door into the lighted interior and fired three quick shots near the man's feet. The messenger dropped his six-gun and held up his hands.

Sam looked over to Seaborn. "Keep watch," he ordered, and then hoisted himself up into the car. "No sense you getting shot over this," he told the messenger, a short, pudgy man with saucer-like eyes. "Now be a good man and open the safe."

"It's not locked," the man said.

Sam shook a flour sack open. He dumped a bundle of cash amounting to three thousand dollars from the safe into the sack. There were no coins or jewelry. Seaborn stood by the open door with his six-gun trained on the messenger while Sam ransacked the car in hope of finding other valuables, like those that had been found in Big Springs. But it was not to be. He was unaware that before the shooting began, the messenger had stashed a bag with fifteen thousand dollars in cash into the cold stove fire box.

Satisfied they had all the loot, Sam made the messenger lie down then took the man's six-gun and a nearby shotgun and flung them out the door. "Lie there for five minutes and you won't get hurt," he told the man. Sam jumped from the car. The three bandits disappeared into the night.

When word of the robbery got back to Denton, Sheriff Egan went into action. He had been suspicious of Sam's activities since his return. Egan went around town checking and sure enough Sam hadn't been seen for two days. His known close companion Frank Jackson was nowhere to be found either. Upon questioning some local merchants and bartenders Egan found that Sam had been passing newly minted twenty dollar gold pieces as payment. A few spot checks indicated that the coins all had the same mint date of 1877 on them. The money alone convinced

Egan that Sam was one of the fugitives of the Big Springs robbery.

Sam had the audacity to convince everyone he had made a big gold mine strike. "He made a big strike all right!" Egan muttered. "Well, he won't get away with it, not this time. I'll find him!" He was angry for allowing Sam to make a fool of him and the entire town.

Sheriff Egan set about to form a posse to hunt Sam Bass down. He addressed a group of men, filling them in on what he felt they needed to know. "The reward of ten thousand dollars for the capture of any of the men who robbed the express car up in Big Springs, Nebraska is still offered by the Union Pacific Railroad. I am certain that Sam Bass is one of those men. There was a train robbery south of Dallas, just last night, and I believe it was done by Bass and others."

Sam, Frank and Seaborn didn't waste any time splitting the loot three ways the night of the robbery, and had brazenly ridden to a Fort Worth Saloon and spent plenty of money celebrating. A day later they rode back to the camp in Cove Hollow.

Meanwhile, the absent Henry Underwood and a man called Arkansas Johnson had ridden into Denton. Back in December Underwood had traveled to Nebraska to visit relatives and had been picked up by a posse because his description was similar to that of Tom Nixon, who was one of the Big Springs bandits. Underwood had been lodged in a jail in Nebraska. The case and the security at the jail were flimsy. Underwood and fellow inmate Arkansas Johnson, a tough as nails man with a reputation of having a fast gun hand, had easily escaped. The two fugitives had stolen some horses and spent the next two weeks riding hard for Texas.

Henry had spoken to Arkansas Johnson about Sam's part in the robbery at Big Springs and of the talk of robbing a train in Texas. They were both eager to get in on the action. When the bartender at the Red Horse Saloon said that he hadn't seen Sam Bass, Frank Jackson or Henderson Murphy the past two nights, Henry Underwood knew that something was up. After noon the next day he and Arkansas Johnson rode to the Murphy cabin on Clear Creek and soon learned where the new outlaw camp was located.

The gang's membership had increased. It didn't take long for Frank Jackson to tell the two new arrivals of the heist of the train and the payoff. "It was the easiest damned money I ever made!" he exclaimed.

Sam wasn't quite as ecstatic as Jackson. He mimicked some of Joel Collins' words: "What we got on that raid is chicken feed compared to what could have been in that express car!"

He was emboldened by the robbery, though,

and assured the others that the next one would pay even better. He coerced the gang to stick up a Texas Pacific train at Eagle Ford six miles from Dallas on April 4th but didn't get much for loot. The safe was empty so they took the pocket money of the messenger and engineer before leaving.

On April 10 the gang struck again at Mesquite. This time the express messenger refused to surrender and open the express car door. Again Sam Bass had to threaten to burn the car with him inside if he didn't do as he was told. After a while the messenger relented and let the bandits in but there was hardly any money in the safe, a mere one hundred fifty dollars. If any thought had been given to getting into the passenger coaches, it was dispelled when the conductor and a host of passengers began shooting through the windows at the bandits. One bullet nipped both of Seaborn Barnes' legs and two other bullets grazed his side and one arm but no one else was touched. A hail of bullets from the robbers' six-guns riddled the coaches and wounded several passengers. Bass called the raid off and the men scrambled for their horses and retreated.

A public protest over the number of train robberies and other lawlessness in northern Texas was brought to the attention of Governor Richard B. Hubbard. The governor reacted right away. In an arranged meeting he commissioned thirty-three year old Junius Peak to the position of Captain in the Texas Rangers. He wanted Peak to raise a special Texas Ranger detachment and bring the train robbing bandits to justice. Junius Peak had served in the Confederate Army and was elected to a four year term as City Marshall of Dallas in 1874, a position he held until sent for by Governor Hubbard.

"You want me to bring in Sam Bass?" Peak asked.

Governor Hubbard put his cigar onto an ashtray on his desk. "Everyone is fed up with Sam Bass and his gang of miscreants. They have robbed too damned many trains. People have had the piss scared out of them. They are tired of it all. The robbery at Mesquite was the last straw, some of the passengers were injured." He hesitated for only a moment before continuing, his voice lowering. "Yes, I want you to bring him in, under his own power or dead and slung over the back of a horse! I really don't care which! And the same goes for any one of his associates."

Thoughtful, Captain Peak scrubbed a weary hand across his chin. "I think you've made your feelings quite clear, Governor."

"Can you do it?" Hubbard asked.

Captain Peak nodded. "Yes, sir, I can. With a full company of Rangers at my disposal, we will run him into ground. And, one way or the other, we *will* bring him in."

The Governor stood and stuck out his hand. "We're counting on you to do this, Captain Peak."

Peak and a complement of Rangers combed the Dallas and Fort Worth area setting up watchful eyes on several watering stations. When nothing occurred, he decided to go north to Denton, Sam Bass' original haunt and one of the last places where he had been seen with his friends. Peak hoped for word regarding Sam's current whereabouts that would lead him to the bandit's gang and ultimate capture.

On April 25th, after a conference with Sheriff Egan, Captain Peak and his Rangers—along with Egan's posse that numbered well over fifty men—took up positions in Cove Hollow where they had discovered the bandits were hiding.

It was slow going for the lawmen as they wrestled their way beneath a waning moon through the brush-filled hillsides, a nighttime trip made necessary by the goal of reaching the camp by daylight. By an earlier agreement, Peak and his Rangers waited on one side of the canyon while Egan and his posse converged on the other.

Egan's men had brush-scratched faces and red-rimmed eyes from their all night traveling. They were tired and wanted coffee and breakfast and were in no mood to do anything but get their guns trained on the bandits. Egan wanted the group to close in on the robbers' camp as one body, but someone in the posse took a shot at one of the bandits who was caught relieving himself. The shot missed the target but woke everyone up to what was happening in both the bandit camp and the assembled posse men. Chaos soon ensued on both sides.

Sam and the other bandits zeroed in on the posses' positions and sent a hail of lead in that direction. There was no order of command as the lawmen hugged the ground and fired blindly in the general direction of the bandits.

"How many you figure is out there?" Henry Underwood asked while taking up a position behind a tree.

"I don't know," Sam said, "but from the firepower it sure looks like a lot!"

Arkansas Johnson fired a rifle shot toward the lawmen. "We ought to get the horses and ride like hell to Mexico!"

Regardless of the outburst by Johnson over the trouble at hand, Sam did not want to show any kind of weakness to the others. "I'm not ready to do that!" he shouted. "Let's just see how this plays out!"

Sam and the others could see there was great confusion among their attackers since the bullets fired in their direction were splattering impotently against the rocky terrain well at their backs and far above them. "Hell, they're just shooting to make noise," Sam declared with great bravado. "Let's get the horses and move on out." The gang took advantage of the situation and broke free of their position. Sam led the way out and was able to lead their escape into the heavy timber and brush of the canyon hillside. The firing continued long after they had ridden away, indicating that the posse and the Rangers were in a battle among themselves, shooting at anything they thought had moved.

When the shooting finally died off, Sheriff Egan found an empty bandit camp. Fortunately no one in the confused assembly had taken a bullet.

Captain Peak and his Rangers were on the other side of the canyon waiting in vain. Afterwards the Rangers and Egan's men came together to scour the bandit camp but they discovered there was nothing there except the bandits' abandoned supplies. Some of the men raided the goods and made coffee and then cooked breakfast. Later, somewhat bewildered by the fruitless events, the lawmen left Cove Hollow canyon.

Sam and the others found vantage points to lounge about while watching until satisfied that all the lawmen had all gone away. When they figured it to be safe, the gang rode down to Henderson Murphy's cabin on Clear Creek and set up a watch. They wrongfully assumed that the posse had given up and would not be back anytime soon. It was but four days later when

Frank Jackson, who was on lookout duty, spotted unnatural movement in the brush and trees on the other side of Clear Creek. When he advised Sam and the others, Henderson Murphy spoke up in objection. "I don't need my cabin shot full of holes and the stock I got killed off!"

Understanding Murphy's concern, Sam nodded. "Let's move out to the barn and get our horses ready. Henderson is right, no sense in getting his place all shot up."

All five gang men made their way to the corral and barn and saddled their horses. No one was particularly worried as there was a long open field between them and their antagonists. The posse men searched for advantaged spots, digging in for what they considered would be a long siege.

"If they shoot from way over there they won't be able to hit a damned thing!" Underwood claimed.

"Let's see if we can get their attention," Sam said and then pointed his Spencer rifle toward the hillside and fired off a shot. There was an immediate shooting barrage from the posse men's rifles at near to four hundred yards distance with similar results to the confrontation a few days before. Sam and the others emptied their rifles toward the location. The posse continued their onslaught with no accuracy, except that one bullet hit the breech of Sam's rifle and knocked it from his hands. Sam was startled and stood still for a moment, and then rallied. "Hell, boys!" he laughed. "They almost got me! Let's get on our way before they get any luckier!" When the five mounted men began to ride away there were a few shots fired at them but neither man nor beast was hit.

Urging their horses to a run, the gang undertook a southern route. Later on they slowed their animals and rode at an almost leisurely pace without further confrontation.

Captain Peak, stung by the gang's twin escapes, dispatched his men to Denton and Dallas saloons in the hopes the bandits would show up for an evening's entertainment. After a few nights and no appearance at any of the establishments where the outlaws usually sought their carnal pleasures, Peak figured the gang had to be hiding out in the outlying areas, abetted—no doubt—by the silence of the inhabitants. The farmers, ranchers and cowhands whose ranges covered that territory knew of every stranger who rode across their land.

Regardless, Peak sent his men into the surrounding countryside to question anyone who may have had contact with the bandits, but it did no good.

All who were questioned were close-mouthed, perhaps having an affinity to Sam Bass as one of their own. It seemed as if they were enjoying the fact they could socialize with such a notorious bandit. It was something they could brag about to their neighbors. One rancher, while being interrogated, declared Sam Bass was being falsely accused. "I always kinda liked Sam, he was helpful when he made his deliveries and he never did any wrong to me." A farmer noted, "Sam Bass, oh hell, he's a good man. He gave my wife a twenty dollar gold piece for a pan of hot biscuits one time when we were flat broke! But that was awhile back, naw, I ain't seen him lately."

Still, Peak arrested anyone who was suspected of harboring the gang. Henderson Murphy along with his son Jim Murphy were taken in to custody though Henderson Murphy had come down with pneumonia and needed rest and care. The worst place that the ailing Henderson could be was in a cold jail cell. After listening to the pleas made by Jim Murphy for the release of his father, Peak decided to use the younger Murphy's loyalty to his father as a method to obtain the information he wanted. It would be a gamble as to whether the distraught youth would balk or go along with what Peak would present.

"If you'll agree to help us capture Sam Bass, we'll drop the charges and allow your father to be released to the care of the town doctor," Peak bargained.

Jim Murphy wanted to be loyal to Sam Bass

and the others, but felt stronger obligations were owed to his father. "How would I do that?" he asked tentatively.

Peak knew he had the boy hooked. "Work undercover. Join the gang if you have to, but you need to keep quiet, as if you don't know anything. If and when Bass returns, you get word to us of his whereabouts and his intentions. I'll give you a telegraph address to notify us of the where and what."

Jim Murphy stared silently at the floor.

"It's either that or you and your father are both headed to prison for harboring fugitives," Peak declared, his tone firm. "I don't think your father would survive very long in that atmosphere."

Visibly shaken, Jim Murphy nodded his understanding.

CHAPTER 9

A few days later Sam and the others had made a camp in a thicket near Hickory Creek which is south of Denton and north of Dallas some dozen miles from either locale.

Sheriff Egan was incensed at the escapes of Sam and the gang members. He had marshaled a large number of men and along with some of Peak's Rangers they combed the country from Cove Hollow to Denton. They were now on the move south of Denton making their clean sweep toward Dallas and intent on running Sam Bass into the ground.

It was near dark when the lawmen found evidence of a hastily abandoned camp at Hickory Creek. Egan ordered the area encircled and began closing in on a thicketed area where he believed the bandits to be hiding. Hampered by the growing darkness a few shots were fired at shadows. In the confusion, Henry Underwood and Frank Jackson's horses bolted away. Once more Sam led the gang on a daring escape that left the frustrated lawmen behind.

Frantic to get out of harm's way, the men had doubled up to ride out of the thicket. Later on and throughout the night they rode some and then would walk awhile, resting the horses before riding again. The gang disappeared from Salt Creek and wandered into neighboring Stephens County. By morning it was evident that the posse had been left behind. Exhausted, they made for a thicket to try and rest up. One of the men stood guard while the others slept. By late afternoon they were determined to travel some more and hopefully find some horses to buy or steal.

It was completely dark when Frank Jackson spotted a dim light in a distant farmhouse. The men approached cautiously and walked into the yard. When no one came out or challenged them, Sam and Arkansas Johnson approached the front door with six-guns in hand. Sam tapped on the door. "Hello, the house. Is anyone there?" There was no answer so Sam tried the door and found it was unlocked. He stood beside the doorway, cautiously turning the knob with one hand, and then pushing the door wide open. Inside, a man lay on the floor. He was snoring loudly, a gallon-sized jug of homebrew sitting nearby. Sam and Arkansas Johnson scanned the single room for others but there wasn't anyone else to be seen. They determined the man on the floor had simply downed enough shine to put himself into a stupor and was sleeping it off.

It wasn't long before the men had their horses stripped of the saddles, led into a corral and properly watered and fed.

Inside the cabin, Sam and the others made

themselves at home cooking bacon, eggs, fried bread and coffee from the sleeping man's larder. They also helped themselves to copious amounts of his homemade whiskey.

Early the next morning Sam sat in a chair smoking a cigarette and sipping coffee when the sleeping man finally aroused. The man sat up and knuckled his eyes with both hands then looked around. His eyes grew larger when he spotted Sam sitting at his table. "Morning," Sam offered. The man nodded and then frowned, perhaps trying to remember the events of the previous night that had led to a stranger being in his house.

Sam stubbed the cigarette out in a sardine can. Then, keeping his tone neutral, he addressed his host. "We came in last night. You were sleeping and we saw fit to not disturb you. We made ourselves a meal and I slept here. The others slept in the barn. Don't worry yourself. We intend to pay for what we use." To prove his point, he dug into his pocket and displayed a twenty dollar gold piece, which he laid on the table beside his plate.

The man rolled over on his hands and knees and then stood. He remained silent while he walked over and took a coffee cup in hand then poured it full. He sipped once and then took a chair at the table. "How many of you are here?" he asked then blew a breath onto the coffee.

"Five, all together," Sam answered.

The man nodded. "You're welcome here, strangers or not. I don't get many visitors."

Sam stuck out a hand. "I'm Sam Bass." He looked into the man's eyes when he gave his name, to see if the man's orbs registered any fear or surprise. They didn't.

"Homer Wiggins," the man announced.

Sam felt the tension leaving his body. "Well, Homer, my friends and I have a small problem. We lost two of our horses a couple nights ago and have been traveling doubled up. So now we are in need of more animals. I looked your stock over, but you only have the one old horse. Any idea as to where we might get a couple saddle mounts?"

Homer supped more coffee. "You fellas on the run from the law?"

Sam nodded. There was no point in denying it. "You might say we're not too welcome over in Denton County. They chased us clear out of the county. Now we're just looking to rest up a bit and find some riding stock."

Homer grinned. "It don't matter to me if you're on the dodge. I've been in that position a time or two myself. You tell your boys to rest easy, won't nobody come out here looking. I've been here nigh on to ten years, preferring to stay away from towns and such. The only travelers that come around are somebody that has lost his way."

"Where are we exactly?" Sam asked.

160

"You're about fifty some miles west of Fort Worth," Homer said. "The nearest town is Breckenridge, about ten, twelve miles northwest of here. I get my supplies from a store over by Caddo, two, three miles distance. As for horses, I'd try the Rocking C ranch, a few miles south of here. If you're in a hurry, you could steal them easy enough but if you got the time and money, ol' Gill Huggins, the ramrod, is a fair man to deal with."

Sam levered himself up from the chair. "We've got time and money, Homer. I don't want to raise anyone's hackles in this county by taking what ain't ours."

After a few days, at Wiggins' urging, Sam and the others settled into Homer Wiggins' place as if it were their own. Henry Underwood and Frank Jackson were able to pick out two horses when they made a trip to the Rocking C. They bought a pair of sorrel geldings and two used saddles from Gill Huggins. The man didn't ask too many questions and seemed quite tickled to sell the animals. Arkansas Johnson and Seaborn Barnes made a trip to the store near Caddo and brought back a supply of cooking goods, tobacco and whiskey. Homer took a special liking to Frank Jackson, perhaps thinking of the young man as one near a lost son's age. To Homer's delight, Frank helped out with the cooking and took over feeding the chickens and gathering the eggs.

The other men spent their days seeing to the care of the horses and lending a hand to Homer with some of the heavier chores that needed doing, changing out a broken wheel on a wagon, patching the cabin roof, fixing a broken corral post and such. After supper their time was spent drinking and playing cards well into the night. It was a respite the gang seemed to relish.

On one such evening of heavy drinking, Homer, Sam, Henry Underwood and Frank Jackson sat around the table playing cards. Sam was the first to break the silence. "How's that new horse you got, Henry?"

Underwood shrugged, his eyes narrowing. "That little sorrel is okay, but he ain't the horse that those bastards took from me!" He scratched the week-old stubble on his chin. "But I guess I don't have a choice in the matter."

Sam looked over to Henry and smiled. "Now that's where you're wrong, Henry. You do have a choice."

Henry eyed him and seemed amused. "How you figure, Sam?"

Sam laid his cards down. "Hell, we could go and take those horses back. That's if we were of a mind to!"

Henry grunted and then smiled. "Why, hell, Sam! I do believe that I've a mind to." He laughed.

Sam grinned. "All right, then. We'll take off

in the morning and go get them. I'll bet you ten dollars that we can take them right out from under their damned noses!"

The next morning Henry Underwood knew it wasn't just whiskey talk when Sam walked out of the cabin carrying his saddle bags, bedroll, and rifle. Henry and the others were quick to get theirs.

In Denton County, folks rumored the gang had fled to Mexico and would likely never be seen in the county again. The fact there had been no activity in the past month seemed to affirm their reasoning.

Early on the morning of June 6th, however, the gang trotted their horses down the streets of Denton. Sam and Frank rushed into Work's Livery while Seaborn Barnes, Arkansas Johnson and Henry Underwood waited outside. It did not take long to find and take back the two horses that the men had lost at Hickory Creek. As the gang galloped away, Underwood shouted gleefully, "Damn them, anyway! They can't steal anything from us that we can't get back!"

In a short time the sleepy town and Sheriff Egan were advised of the gang's raid. Egan was beside himself with anger. He rousted a posse and took immediate pursuit. The posse dogged the gang for three full days and nights giving no respite to the bandits. Twice the posse came close enough to exchange gunshots with the bandits only to find out afterwards that the gang had escaped again and ridden away, heading in a southwest direction.

Late in the afternoon of the third day, Sam and the gang members were still under constant pressure by the harassing posse. Sam thought they had given the lawmen the slip and halted for a rest. The weary men dismounted and were preparing to make camp at Salt Creek, hopeful for a respite. But that idea was short-lived as suddenly Peak's Rangers almost rode in on top of them. Gunfire broke out immediately. Henry Underwood made a mad dash for the horses and managed to mount his animal and lead the other horses to a timbered area while his companions sent a hail of bullets toward the Rangers. Arkansas Johnson stood his ground, pulled his six-gun and fired into the Rangers' midst. The Rangers returned a murderous fire. This time a Ranger's bullet found Johnson, striking the man in the chest and killing him instantly. The Rangers advanced and almost rode on top of Henry Underwood. Under a hail of flying lead, Henry Underwood left the gang's horses and fled. He managed to escape to parts unknown.

Sam Bass, Frank Jackson and Seaborn Barnes, caught without mounts, could only flee down the creek on foot. As they skulked away from the Rangers, it was apparent their only salvation would be the approaching darkness. So they waited, hopeful of not being found. Later on when it was fully dark, the three were able to elude the lawmen again but this time they were afoot. Their horses had been lost to the Rangers.

The three men knew that Arkansas Johnson had been killed in the incident but weren't sure of Henry Underwood's fate, if he had escaped or had been slain.

It took two days of hiking for the men before they stole some horses from a farmer's corral. Sam and Frank Jackson were then able to make their way north and back to Cove Hollow. Seaborn Barnes had split off and headed to his home which was a few miles north of Dallas.

Back at the Murphy cabin in Cove Hollow both the Murphys were surprised that Sam would dare come back since the many lawmen surely had the roads staked out. Sam had banked on the fact the authorities would figure it would be the last place he would go, and it was easy enough to get past prying eyes in darkness. Cove Hollow was the closest thing Sam had to a home and it was a focal point. In the lamplight of the cabin, Sam was elated when Jim Murphy indicated he would like to be a part of the gang. Previously Jim had declined membership. He'd thought what Sam and the others were doing was exciting, but had never held the idea of stealing as his chosen profession. Besides, he did not have the temperament or nerve to take those kind of risks.

But things were different now, and he'd made a choice.

Jim Murphy did not harbor the grand illusions about quick riches Sam and the others seemed to possess. He had heard stories about others who had been shot or killed while doing robberies, and the majority of those men had robbed out of desperation and need. Sam, however, with all the money he threw around, gave the impression he enjoyed robbing and being chased.

And that part was true, Jim reflected. Sam was in his element, getting a rush from both robbing *and* running. The young man believed he was a good leader, and he was intent on filling the void that Joel Collins had left, all the time basking in the glory of having men look to him for direction.

In truth, Jim Murphy did not want to join the gang. But he had no choice. The threat of incarceration hung over his father like a dark cloud, the situation made even more intense by the older man's fragile health. Deep inside, Jim knew he would do whatever he had to do to save his father, no matter the cost.

So he tried, as best he could, to act enthusiastic enough to convince Sam he was eager to join in the game. He flattered, he cajoled, and in the end the ploy worked. Sam accepted the young man into the gang, congratulating himself that he had not only found a convert, but had increased the ranks in the gang that had been left short-handed by the losses of Henry Underwood and Arkansas Johnson.

Sam had always liked both Murphys. Henderson would always tell you exactly what he had on his mind and Sam respected him for his frankness. Jim was young and impressionable. Sam judged him to be about Frank Jackson's age, which was twenty. That put both boys seven years younger than his own age of almost twenty-seven, young enough to bow to his will and to follow his orders.

As instructed by Ranger Captain Peak, Jim Murphy set out on his assigned task to find out when and where Sam was going to lead the gang on their next strike, and to somehow get word back to the Ranger. Murphy realized he needed to be very careful. After considerable thought, he decided to make a suggestion to Sam. He approached the bandit and laid out his thoughts. "You know, Sam," he started, "the law is everywhere between here and Dallas. I figure that they're lying in wait at the train water stops, and the railroad has most likely put on extra guards, too. Maybe it's time to do something different, something they aren't expecting."

Sam's attention was on young Murphy. "And what would that be?"

Murphy smiled. "Go south, clear on out of the county where the law isn't all fired up and just waiting for you to make another move. Only this time, stay away from the railroad and maybe rob a bank!"

Sam's head canted as he considered the younger man's words. He smiled. "I like it, Jim." He clapped the boy on the back. "You've got a good head on your shoulders."

It was near daylight when Sam, Frank Jackson and Jim Murphy rode into the yard of Seaborn Barnes' small farm just north of Dallas. Seaborn moved out to greet the men, his face clearly showing surprise as he spied Jim Murphy. Reaching out to stroke the neck of Murphy's horse, he stared up at the ride. "So, the law ran you and your dad in, then let both of you go, uh?"

Jim Murphy shifted uncomfortably in his saddle, averting his eyes for a moment as he regained control. "They didn't have anything on us," he said. "Hell, we didn't do anything wrong, so they had to let us go." Murphy was hopeful his answer would satisfy Seaborn, as well as his companions, who appeared to be listening closely to what he was saying.

Seaborn himself had been arrested before and was suspicious of Jim's claims they were allowed to go home without being charged. He waited to voice his opinion until Murphy led his horse across the yard to the watering trough, and then made his thoughts known. "I don't trust Murphy, Sam," he began, keeping his voice low. "I never thought that he or his dad had the sand to have a part in something like this. I've seen him around town before, but I never seen the kid stand up to anyone. He always stood back as if he expected his pa to take care of things." Staring across to where Murphy was watering his horse, he shook his head. "The law never let me go that easy."

Angry, Sam glared at Seaborn. "You believe he would turn on us?"

Seaborn shrugged, "Just an observation, that's all. I don't know if he's dependable."

Frank Jackson had been listening to the exchange between Sam and Seaborn. He decided to toss in his two cents. "I've known Jim Murphy most of my life," he ventured, his tone confrontational. "We grew up together. He wouldn't do anything to bring harm to any of us."

Seaborn's tone matched Jackson. "Well if he does, I'll kill him!"

The four gang members rested at Barnes' cabin until dark and then rode straight south, conscious of the fact that a roaming posse could still be about. They camped when daylight came then proceeded again at dark.

In two nights they had covered around fifty miles, and it was a little before mid-day when they arrived just outside the town of Waco. Sam handed out twenty dollar gold pieces to the men to finance their activities and to pay for their lodgings. "I think we left the law behind in Denton County," he declared, doling out the coins. "So there's no reason why we can't just rest up a couple days and see how things go."

They entered town two at a time, meeting up later that night at a corner card table in Mica's Saloon. After several drinks, the conversation turned to some serious planning for robbing the bank there in Waco. It seemed an ideal setting, a small town with limited law enforcement, just a city marshal as far as they had seen.

Seaborn Barnes brought up the idea of stealing some horses so that they would have fresh mounts if a posse took after them.

Jim Murphy knew he would not have the opportunity to get word to the authorities in time to inform them of the gang's intentions and decided to voice his disapproval of the plan. "I don't think stealing horses is such a good idea," he reasoned. "Why get the local law stirred up or put them on the alert?" Certain they would get caught or killed, he implored Sam to not steal any horses or rob the local bank. "I think we should go further south," he suggested, "some place not so close to home."

Sam spent the night thinking over Murphy's advice. The next morning after breakfast, he pulled the younger man aside and voiced his decision. "If you think there is too much danger here, Jim, we won't hit the bank. We'll go wherever you say."

Murphy answered right away. "I was talking to a fella last night that said on down south is a little town called Round Rock. He said it was a busy cattle town."

Seaborn, who had joined the pair, spoke up. "I've been there before and there is a bank there. I know that because I helped herd some cattle through there once. I spent some time in the Left Hand Saloon. Fella that owned the place didn't have a left hand, so he called the saloon his left hand." He paused to concentrate on the cigarette he was rolling. "Town's small," he said, spitting a flake of loose tobacco, "and it's quiet. Don't think they got much in the way of a lawman, either."

Sam nodded. "Fair enough," he said. "We'll go on down there."

The next morning was Sunday, it was quiet in Waco. The four men were drinking coffee in the hotel café. Jim Murphy stood up and stretched. "I need to check on my horse. He's been favoring a front leg," he said, and then left.

Murphy did go to the livery where his horse was stabled, but not before making a surreptitious detour into the telegraph office and sending a wire to the Grayson County Sheriff's office. He informed the sheriff the bank in Round Rock, a little town twenty miles north of Austin, would be robbed later that week.

Jim then went to the livery, making a fuss over

171

his horse's hoof and asking the stableman to take a look. When nothing wrong was found with the animal, Jim rejoined the others. He was hopeful he was beyond anyone's suspicion as no one said anything other than Sam.

"How's the horse?" Sam asked affably.

Acting embarrassed, Murphy shrugged. "The stableman said it should be fine, that it was probably just a stone bruise," he replied. The confession brought a round of good-natured teasing and laughter from the older men, about how the young man was a worrywart and prone to acting like a mother hen.

The gang stayed in town until the next morning before moving on south. They arrived outside Round Rock three days later and set up camp about a mile from town, near a cemetery. Their next move was to head into town to check things out. Once their curiosity was satisfied, they returned to their campsite.

Sam gathered the men around him, and laid out his plans. "We'll sleep here, but I see no reason we can't go into town as long as we don't draw any attention to ourselves," he continued. "I sure could use a shave, a meal and a beer, maybe a hand or two of poker. Seaborn says there's no guns allowed in town, so we need to keep them out of sight." He took his gun belt off and stuffed it in his saddle bag, but shoved the six-gun in his belt under his jacket. Then he and Seaborn mounted and rode to town. It had been decided Frank Jackson and Jim Murphy would join them later.

The men gravitated naturally away from the higher class end of town where the bank was, and on to the lower end of town where the saloons were. Jim Murphy and Frank Jackson went into Mary's Café and had apple pie and coffee while Sam and Seaborn walked the streets to get a better feel for the town.

Round Rock was a small town that had sprung up along the Chisholm Trail, so called because of a large round-anvil shaped rock in the middle of Brushy Creek where there was a low water crossing for horses and cattle alike. It became a good overnight stopping spot for cattlemen herding their cattle north. Like other settlements along the Chisholm, the only commerce came from nearby cattle ranches or from those driving herds through the area.

In the past few days, however, the town had begun to fill with Rangers. Major John B. Jones had been notified by the Grayson County Sheriff of the impending robbery of the Williamson County Bank. Ranger Captain Peak was also informed of the news but decided to wait in Denton in case this was merely a ruse. He in turn told Sheriff Egan, and both lawmen agreed that the distance was too far away to attempt an assault.

It was a bright Friday afternoon when several Rangers began congregating at the railroad depot in Round Rock. When they dispersed, some walked the streets while others entered businesses. Ranger Sergeant Richard Ware stepped into a barber shop to get a shave. Ranger George Herold was browsing next door in a saddler's shop. Major Jones went into the telegraph office. It was late in the week and no gang activities had been reported since he had received the telegraph from the Grayson County Sheriff this Sunday past. Jones wondered if the information provided to him had been false.

After two days of lounging at their campsite the four gang members rode toward town in the late afternoon to buy some tobacco and get a last look at the town's layout before carrying out the robbery, which would occur the next day. When they came to the edge of town, Jim Murphy called out to Sam. "I don't need anything at the store so I think I'll go on down to the café and see if they got any more of that apple pie. Are you coming with me, Frank?"

Frank Jackson shook his head. "Nah, I'll go on to the store with Sam and Seaborn."

Jim Murphy rode on down the street as Sam, Seaborn, and Frank walked their horses to a hitch rack in the alley beside Henry Kopel's general store. The three men dismounted, tied their reins to the hitch rail and then walked through the alley onto the street. They turned left and went through the front door of Kopel's store.

Deputy Sheriff Moore, who had ridden into town with Major Jones, was across the street and had watched when the three men rode in. He stepped inside the sheriff's office and addressed Deputy Sheriff Grimes, the resident Williamson County deputy. "I think one of those fellows that just went into Kopel's store has a pistol under his jacket."

Grimes sat upright in his chair and then stood and walked to the window to look outside. "Let's go over and see," he said. The two lawmen left the office and walked across the street. Deputy Moore waited outside to roll a smoke while Grimes crossed the threshold into Kopel's store.

Sam, Frank, and Seaborn were standing in front of the counter when the lawman came in. Grimes stopped six feet behind them and asked, "Are any of you men carrying pistols?"

The three bandits turned to face Grimes. Seaborn had his hand under his coat. "Yes, we have guns," Sam said, "but . . ." He was cut off in mid-sentence when Seaborn pulled his six-gun out and fired a shot into Grimes' stomach. Deputy Grimes was in the act of reaching for his holstered six-gun when Seaborn shot him again.

Sam and Frank, startled by the two pistol shots, instinctively snaked out their six-guns and began shooting as well. Deputy Grimes, riddled with bullets, fell to the floor dead. When the first shot was fired, Deputy Moore, standing outside the store, immediately pulled his six-gun and opened the door. He fired five shots into the smoke-filled room before falling to the floor with a bullet in his chest. One of Moore's bullets had struck Sam in his gun hand, lopping both middle fingers off. The three bandits lunged for the door.

Ranger Ware was sitting in a barber's chair getting a shave when the shooting started. Ware bolted out of the chair and ran into the street with the soap on his face, his weapon drawn.

When he located the bandits a hundred paces down and across the street, Ware began firing his six-gun at them. Ranger George Herold rushed out of the saddle shop and began blazing away at the outlaws as well. Return fire from the bandits on the run riddled the air. Major Jones hurried out of the telegraph office and was only able to get off one shot at the bandits before they ducked around the corner of the store.

Sam, Frank, and Seaborn ran down the alley where their horses were tethered. Ranger Ware had run down the street far enough to peek into the alley. He was able to take aim at the three escaping men and fire. One bullet found its mark, Seaborn Barnes was hit in midstride, shot in the back of the head. He died where he fell. Nearby Ranger Herold turned his six-gun on the other two, Sam and Frank. Sam took a bullet to his lower back just as he reached his horse. He collapsed against the horse's flank. Frank Jackson saw that Sam was hit and came to help Sam into the saddle before mounting his own horse. Jackson emptied his six-gun in the direction of the Rangers then tried as best he could to hold Sam in the saddle as he urged the horses away. Bullets were flying around the two men as they fled town. The run lasted only a short time before Sam began to fall out of the saddle. Frank Jackson was able to maneuver the horses to a wooded area beside an open field. He helped Sam down and propped him upright against an oak tree.

Sam knew he had been badly wounded by the shot to his back. Pain and blood loss had sapped his strength. His face was drained of color and he spoke in a halting voice, "You got to ride on . . . Frank!" he urged his younger companion.

Frank's face was flushed red and his eyes were wide with apprehension. He took a deep breath, trying to sort out the conflicting urges inside him. He did not want to abandon Sam and leave him alone to deal with the pursuing lawmen, but common sense told him he needed to get away. Feelings of loyalty were overwhelming the youth: Sam was his friend, they had ridden together, faced danger together and he would not leave Sam to the fates. Frank shook his head. "I'm staying with you, Sam!"

Grimacing in pain, Sam shook his head. "No, no, I want you to go!" he gasped. He reached out to clutch Jackson's arm. "They'll shoot you, too! I'm done for, Frank," he ground out. "I can't ride any more. Take my guns and my horse. He's faster than yours. You've got to get away!" Sam passed his six-gun to Frank with his uninjured left hand. "Now go! Go!"

Sam was so insistent that Frank finally relented. He abruptly stood. "All right, Sam, if that's what you want, I'll go."

Sam nodded. "That's what I want, Frank," he said softly. "They'll be here soon. Now go!"

Frank reloaded his six-gun and then mounted Sam's horse. He paused to look down at Sam through tear-filled eyes and jerked the reins to turn the horse about. He kicked the big bay to a run and rode off.

Contrary to Sam's belief, the lawmen did not mount an immediate pursuit. When the Rangers had all gotten together in conference, Major Jones announced, "We're not sure of the number of men in that gang. We saw only three in town but there's a good chance that there are more at a camp nearby. Those men are desperate and will shoot to kill. They already killed Deputy Grimes, and badly wounded Deputy Moore. It'll be dark soon and I don't want any other lawman getting killed or maimed. We'll get ourselves organized and begin the hunt at first light. I'll get on the telegraph and we'll have an army of men on the move tonight. Those bastards are not going to get away!"

As soon as Jim Murphy heard the noise of the shots coming from up the street, he figured that it involved Sam and the others and that something had gone wrong. He was immediately torn as to what to do. If Sam and the others had been recognized then he didn't want to go running up there and get into the middle of the confrontation, nor did he want to get shot by the lawmen. It hit him then, that since he had been the one who had set the whole thing up, it wouldn't take much for Sam and the others to put the pieces together and figure out what he had done. His chances of getting shot had increased twofold: the Rangers or his former friends, either faction could and would be capable of taking his life.

By the time the shooting had ended there were plenty of excited voices coming from the other end of town. Murphy, standing next to his horse and contemplating whether to mount and ride to safety or stay where he was, spotted a man walking hurriedly along the boardwalk in his direction.

Feigning ignorance, he called out to the man. "What was all the shooting about?"

The stranger hesitated. "The deputy's been killed, and they think it was the Bass gang!" he blurted breathlessly. "One of the gang was killed too!"

Jim Murphy spent an agonizing ten minutes aimlessly walking the streets before deciding it was time to make his presence known. After all, it was done! Jim Murphy could now come out of hiding. He was grim-faced as he walked into the sheriff's office where Major Jones and two other Rangers had just assembled. The three men glared dourly when he stepped through the door. He was uneasy when he announced, "I'm Jim Murphy, the one that sent the telegram about the gang!"

Major Jones rose up from behind a desk. He eyed the young man with scrutiny then held an open hand palm up in a gesture of uncertainty. "I never received a telegram from anybody but the Grayson county sheriff. He said there was someone working undercover as an informant. Would that be you?"

Jim Murphy nodded. "Yes, that would be me."

One of the Rangers stepped forward and took Murphy's pistol from his waistband.

"You know who the others are then?" Jones asked.

Murphy nodded again.

"Good," Jones said. "Then you won't have any problem identifying the one member of the gang who didn't escape town."

Jim Murphy was accompanied by the Major and

the other two Rangers to where Seaborn Barnes still lay. Barnes' body was lying on its back, eyes open in a glassy death stare. Jim Murphy took one look and murmured, "That's Seaborn Barnes. He was one of the Bass gang."

Major Jones grimaced. "How many more are there?"

Murphy's chin dropped against his chest, his gaze still locked on the still body of Seaborn Barnes. "Two more is all," he answered. "Sam Bass and Frank Jackson."

Major Jones seemed astonished. "Just Bass and one other? Hell, we thought there might be a dozen or more! Well, one of them got himself wounded while running away, that's according to a couple of our men. I'm surprised that anyone could survive that hail of lead that was thrown at them! Nevertheless, the fact that one of them is wounded is going to slow them down!"

"What do you want me to do?" Jim Murphy asked.

Major Jones looked to Murphy. "Right now nothing. I'm ordering that you be held in our protective custody until the others are caught and this matter is resolved. If those other two got wind of you coming forward they most likely wouldn't hesitate to gun you down."

At first light, the hunt began in earnest. The Rangers spread out to make a sweep northwest of town, where the bandits had fled. They had traveled less than a mile when two Rangers spotted a man sitting against an oak tree on the edge of an open field. They approached on foot, with six-guns drawn.

When Sam saw them, he held a hand up. "Don't shoot," he said in a weak voice. "I am the one you are looking for. I am Sam Bass."

A wagon was brought from town and Sam was loaded into the wagon bed. He was taken to a doctor's office in town. Doctor Mortimer Davis examined Sam and did what he could to staunch the seeping of blood from the wounds. He discovered that the bullet had come out near Sam's groin at an inordinate angle. Dr. Davis thought it odd that it appeared there were two entry wounds in the same hole in Sam's back. The doctor examined the cartridge belt Sam had been wearing and determined that the bullet had first struck a cartridge and split apart. Part of the bullet had come out in the groin area and the other part had taken an upward angle and was still inside Sam's body. Sam was so weak from trauma and the great loss of blood that the doctor deferred any probing for the bullet fragments. He attended the body wounds and then bandaged where Sam's two missing fingers had been blown off.

When Major Jones came in to see if he could interrogate his prisoner, Dr. Davis looked at the senior Ranger then cast his eyes to the floor and shook his head from side to side. "He might last the day out, but I wouldn't count on it."

Major Jones stepped to Sam's bedside and looked down at the young man's face. He asked, "Sam, are you awake?"

Sam was lying on his back. His eyes fluttered open upon hearing the voice. His head ached and his vision was bleared and fuzzy, not allowing any recognition of who was there. "Where am I?" he asked.

Major Jones pulled up a chair and sat. "You're at the doctor's office." The Major waited a moment, considering his next words. "You've been shot pretty bad, Sam. One of our men, Deputy Grimes, was killed over at the store. Can you tell me who shot him?"

Sam swallowed. "I never intended to hurt anyone, and if it was my bullet that killed the deputy, then it's the first man that I ever killed."

Major Jones pushed for more. "We both know that your robbing days are over, Sam, but I don't believe that you'll hang. Can you tell me where Frank Jackson went? There's no need for him to be chased and shot, just taken into custody for his own good. We need to put this whole thing to rest."

Sam blinked his eyes. "I won't hang because you know I'm going to die. I don't know where Frank went, I've got nothing more to say."

Major Jones left when Sam closed his eyes. He figured to let the man rest some then maybe question him later.

Sam did make it through the night and on into the next day which happened to be his 27th birthday. By noon his condition had grown worse. The doctor had summoned Major Jones.

When Major Jones walked in, the doctor let him know his prognosis. "It'll be any time now."

Major Jones approached Sam's bedside, hopeful to make one last plea. "Sam, I think you know you don't have long. Why won't you tell me of Frank Jackson's whereabouts?"

Sam answered in a subdued, halting voice that was barely audible. "Because it is ag'in my profession to blow on my pals. If a man knows anything then he ought to die with it!"

Major Jones stared at Sam. "Even if it might save a man's life?"

Sam rolled his head to look away from Major Jones without responding.

At four o'clock Dr. Davis sent a messenger to tell Major Jones that Sam Bass had died.

EPILOGUE

The fate of the six men who held up and robbed Express #4 in Big Springs, Nebraska has only been partially brought to light. Joel Collins and John (Skeeter) Wilcox died in the shootout on the plains of Kansas eight days after the robbery. Willie Jacobs and Tom Nixon escaped to eastern Nebraska where they split. Tom Nixon went north into Canada and disappeared.

Willie Jacobs was intent on making it to his home farm in northern Missouri near the town of Mexico. On October 14th, less than thirty days after the robbery at Big Springs, Willie Jacobs was shot by a waiting sheriff's posse and later died from his wounds. Of the loot he carried, only about two thousand eight hundred dollars was recovered.

Sam Bass and Jack Davis made it back to Texas where they split up. Jack Davis escaped to New Orleans and possibly South America. His whereabouts remains a mystery.

Sam Bass celebrated his return to Denton in revelry. It was but a short time later that he formed a gang of his own to lead.

Of the six men in the newly formed Bass gang in Texas, Arkansas Johnson was gunned down in the thickets in Salt Creek. Henry Underwood escaped and was never heard from again, suggesting that he most likely changed his name and left the Denton area for good, possibly back to his relatives in Nebraska.

Seaborn Barnes was killed in the alley next to Kopel's store in Round Rock.

Sam Bass died from his gunshot wounds two days after the shooting in Round Rock. Ironically, Sam's funeral was similar to that of his original mentor, Claude Radkin. The attendees would have been the gravediggers only, except after they had loaded Sam's pine coffin in a wagon and headed to the gravesite they passed by a Methodist minister's house on the way. The minister joined in and conducted a Christian funeral for the former bandit.

Afterwards a woman working in a cotton field nearby observed that a young man on a big bay horse came to the gravesite. He dismounted and stood there for a moment then threw a clod of dirt onto the grave, mounted the horse, and left. It may have been that Frank Jackson, under Sam Bass' tutelage, had learned ways to elude a posse and had come back to pay a final tribute to his leader. One thing is for sure. Jackson managed to escape the Rangers' search of the surrounding areas. It's possible he rode north back to Homer Wiggins' place in Stephens County or changed his name and moved to some other locale. Perhaps Sam, lying mortally wounded, when he dismissed

Jackson from his side in the woods, had told the youth the whereabouts of his remaining share of the Big Springs robbery. Sam had less than one hundred dollars in his pockets when searched. Frank Jackson was not seen again.

Jim Murphy went back to his father's place near Cove Hollow. He died less than a year later from ingesting poison. Some say he took the poison voluntarily, out of remorse. Others speculate it was the work of Frank Jackson avenging the death of Sam Bass.

The one certain thing is that Sam Bass and his legacy of banditry had passed into history.

ABOUT THE AUTHOR

Jerry Guin is best known as a short story writer with 28 to his credit. His book, *Trail Dust* captures 12 of those stories.

Jerry has written *Matsutake Mushroom*, a nature guide book. He wrote his first western novel, *Drover's Vendetta*, in 2011, followed by *Drover's Bounty*, a Black Horse Western released by Robert Hale Ltd. August 30, 2013.

He had stories appear in the following anthologies: *Outlaws and Lawmen* by La Frontera publishing and *Six-Guns and Slay Bells, A Creepy Cowboy Christmas* by Western Fictioneers. Also through Western Fictioneers, Jerry wrote chapter one of *Wolf Creek, Dog Leg City, Book 3*.

Jerry lives in the extreme Northern California community of Salyer with his wife Ginny.

Books are produced in the United States using U.S.-based materials

Books are printed using a revolutionary new process called THINKtech™ that lowers energy usage by 70% and increases overall quality

Books are durable and flexible because of Smyth-sewing

Paper is sourced using environmentally responsible foresting methods and the paper is acid-free

Center Point Large Print
600 Brooks Road / PO Box 1
Thorndike, ME 04986-0001 USA

(207) 568-3717

US & Canada:
1 800 929-9108
www.centerpointlargeprint.com